"What are you doing in my apartment?"

She turned to face him then, her blouse tightly balled in one hand, her bra wet and now transparent. Beads of water glistening, rolling down over her stomach.

"Your door was open."

Peter's mind was racing now, thinking how good she looked, the woman so in his thoughts, the woman he was writing about now . . .

"How did you even know where I lived?" he asked.

"You told me, remember? Your name's on the buzzer." She reached up to touch his face. "I wanted to see you again, Peter."

He turned in exasperation, pulling back, looking away. "Look," he said. "What happened in Madison was . . ."

"Just the beginning," she said.

I'm back.

UNWOUND

Jonathan Baine

AN ONYX BOOK

ONYX
Published by New American Library, a division of
Penguin Group (USA) Inc., 375 Hudson Street,
New York, New York 10014, USA
Penguin Group (Canada), 90 Eglinton Avenue East, Suite 700, Toronto,
Ontario M4P 2Y3, Canada (a division of Pearson Penguin Canada Inc.)
Penguin Books Ltd., 80 Strand, London WC2R 0RL, England
Penguin Ireland, 25 St. Stephen's Green, Dublin 2,
Ireland (a division of Penguin Books Ltd.)
Penguin Group (Australia), 250 Camberwell Road, Camberwell, Victoria 3124,
Australia (a division of Pearson Australia Group Pty. Ltd.)
Penguin Books India Pvt. Ltd., 11 Community Centre, Panchsheel Park,
New Delhi - 110 017, India
Penguin Group (NZ), cnr Airborne and Rosedale Roads, Albany,
Auckland 1310, New Zealand (a division of Pearson New Zealand Ltd.)
Penguin Books (South Africa) (Pty.) Ltd., 24 Sturdee Avenue,
Rosebank, Johannesburg 2196, South Africa

Penguin Books Ltd., Registered Offices:
80 Strand, London WC2R 0RL, England

First published by Onyx, an imprint of New American Library,
a division of Penguin Group (USA) Inc.

First Printing, January 2007
10 9 8 7 6 5 4 3 2 1

Copyright © Gorman Bechard, 2007
All rights reserved

 REGISTERED TRADEMARK—MARCA REGISTRADA

Printed in the United States of America

PUBLISHER'S NOTE
This is a work of fiction. Names, characters, places, and incidents either are the
product of the author's imagination or are used fictitiously, and any resem-
blance to actual persons, living or dead, business establishments, events, or lo-
cales is entirely coincidental.
    The publisher does not have any control over and does not assume any re-
sponsibility for author or third-party Web sites or their content.

For Kristine,
every word, always, for you

Acknowledgments

Acknowledgments first to Nicole Siggins and Rob Matsushita, as well as everyone involved at the Broom Street Theatre in Madison, Wisconsin, for unknowingly planting the seed that would bloom into this tale.

To my trusted readers of early drafts, my purveyors of tough love, both friends, in one case, a good neighbor, Fred Russo, in the other, my agent for life, Matthew Bialer.

To my many friends, associates, and family members who inspire in so many incalculable ways: Kristine, Frank Loftus, Ashley McGarry, Margaret Laney, Bob Dixon, Deanna Schuppel, Tricia Mara, Betcee May, Casey & Kate Prestwood, Kathy Milani, Steve Manzi, Stephen Handwerk (designsinflash.com), Jeff Petrin, Maya Rossi, Jessica Bohl, Richard Brundage, Anna Bierhaus, William Roberts, Deb & Stan & Kaelee, Gary Bechard, Richard & Kathy Covello, Jeff & Paula & Joe & Logan & Mac, John & Raynell & John-John & Jenna, Rick & Hope & Rickie & Jessica,

Andrew I. Schaffer, Mike Gilio, Marie Montgomery, Kate Geruntho, Bob & Milly, Mary Russo, Nathan Rohn, Chris Gombos, Gene Lynch, Todd Fay, Tom Campbell, Amie Couchon, Tanya Brunet, Kathleen Cei, Christopher Arnott, Jon Cooper, Nick R. Scalia, Pat Ferrucci, Vinnie Penn, my readers, and anyone else who's offered support, encouragement, and friendship over the years.

To my Hollywood agent, Candace Lake.

To Claire Zion and the folks at NAL, for believing in this book.

To Willoughby's, for providing the coffee.

To Sally's, Olde World, Modern, and Pepe's, for providing the nourishment.

To my dogs, Kilgore Trout, Phoebe Caulfield, and the late Casey, who died right after I completed this book. You've inspired me more than you can ever understand.

CASEY
January 13, 1994–March 12, 2006
May there be plenty of treats and
tennis balls, a warm fireplace,
and a big soft couch . . .
wherever you are, girl.
Rest in Peace.

And last, there's the music playing in the background as I write and rewrite. And I'd be lying if I didn't admit that every book starts with one song, the same song, "Here Comes a Regular" by the Replacements. And when its final notes faded, these were waiting to fill the silence: Bright Eyes, Crooked Fingers, the Archers of Loaf, Matt Ryan, Wilco, Lucinda Williams, Neutral Milk Hotel, and also some old Rod Stewart and the Faces thrown in there for good measure this time around.

I thank you all.

PART ONE

Angel Prologue

She put the lipstick on last, amused that it was always what would come off first, before even the most obvious stitch of clothing. On lips sometimes, or a cheek, or less likely a starched white collar. But usually, at least half the time, it found its way elsewhere, a marking, well-charted territory, a bright red macho cock-ring tattoo.

Angel took one last look at her reflection in the compact mirror—perfect!—before snapping it shut, that whoosh, a vapor lock, as if part of her soul had been forever relinquished to the other side. She slipped the jewel-encrusted token—anything encrusted with jewels had better damn well be a token of appreciation, if nothing else—into her large black purse. And tugging on the hem of the small black dress, emphasis on small, making sure there were no wrinkles, not that there was even enough material to wrinkle, she sat back, sinking into the luxury of her ride, enjoying the view from the backseat of the stretch Mercedes as it made its way from Manhattan over the Brooklyn Bridge.

It was always Christmas at the River Café, as if Santa Claus's New York mistress had designed the perfect little hideaway for her annual rendezvous with the fat man. Perhaps that was why it left Angel a little light-headed, like from spiked eggnog; perhaps it was why he always took her there. That twinkle of lights overhead and all around, their reflections playing leapfrog on the East River with those reflections from the island across the way. A watery school yard of light and joy.

Angel sauntered past the maître d', a stop, a slight flip of her hair over her right shoulder, the fingers of her right hand lingering there, then brushing past her neck, down between her breasts. Her hair the perfect length, so that when she disrobed there was always a little mystery left. Thick, so that you could get lost in it, with just the slightest wave. It smelled of papaya and pineapple, a tropical combo that made Angel think of beaches and sunset, and the color, a dark brown, bordering almost on black. No matter the sayings, when a man made love to a blonde, he was fantasizing about a brunette.

Most of them in the room turned now, the men staring, wanting; she'd go as far as to suggest needing. A few getting those looks of annoyance from their dates, especially the older men, the harsh whispers of, "You're old enough to be her father"—or grandfather, in a few of the cases.

But only one man stood. Richard. Tall, handsome Richard. Rich beyond all need Richard. Insecure, needy Richard.

Smiling, her gaze sweeping the floor as if too excited to meet his, Angel stepped forward, the male eyes following her as she crossed the restaurant and leaned up into his arms. They kissed, his breath already sweet from wine and expectations.

"If only you knew the effect you had on me," he said.

"What makes you think I don't?" she replied.

*   *   *

Her panties came off in the elevator, somewhere between the twenty-ninth and thirty-third floors, on their way to forty-eight. Her lipstick had been long lost on the limo ride there—barely, as Richard could hardly contain his excitement. Perhaps it was the way she stared up into his eyes. They all seemed to like that. She'd ask why, but talking wasn't a turn-on. Unless they were doing the talking, about their day, their conquests, their lives . . . their wives. It was her job to listen.

Falling into his apartment, oblivious to everything but his desire, Richard pressed Angel up against a window. They were part of the skyline now, the cold startling and exquisite against her skin. If nipples could cut glass they'd be dead, having fallen through, taking the endless view with them.

Two hours later, precisely, after wine and having satisfied Richard again, the first time as an appetizer, this time for dessert—but no lipstick ring, no lipstick left—Angel told him it was time for her to go. Pulling herself from his arms, standing, stepping into the black dress, pulling it up against his wishes, slowly, as if to leave him wanting more. Her eyes landed for a beat on a framed photo, Richard and a blonde, wife number two.

"Can I see you tomorrow?" he asked, his hands persistent. "My wife's away this weekend."

"I can't, baby," Angel replied, looking now into his face, forcing a sweet smile, gently removing his hands from between her legs. "You know I'm booked."

"But . . ."

She quieted his protest by sucking once on each of his fingers.

"Your night is Friday," she said. "It always will be."

Failing to hide the disappointment, Richard lifted his

slacks from a jumbled puddle of black Armani on the floor, retrieving his wallet and from it twenty-five crisp hundred-dollar bills, which he folded in half, then pressed into the palm of Angel's hand. It was her fee for two hours, plus a twenty-five-percent tip. She could have charged him more for her company during dinner. But Richard was a regular. And Angel liked to eat.

She thanked him with a soft kiss.

"Next Friday, then," he said.

"Of course," she replied.

Angel made it home five minutes before her eleven p.m. weekend-night curfew, the limo having dropped her off a block east of the West Village apartment in which she lived. The small black dress was rolled now into the corner of her oversize bag, replaced by low-cut jeans and a belly shirt. Her hair was pulled back into a ponytail. Jelly bracelets dangled from her left wrist. Her lipstick was nothing more than strawberry-flavored Chap Stick.

Entering the two-bedroom apartment as she always did on Friday or Saturday nights after work, Angel headed right for the kitchen—the fridge, to be specific—walking past her mom, who sat on the living room sofa watching the local news.

"How was the movie?" her mom asked.

"Good," Angel yelled from the other room, a safe enough response, as she made a face, coming up with nothing more than a bottle of springwater, wishing she had ordered the tiramisu at the River Café. Then, popping her head back into the room: "I'm going to bed."

"Good night," her mom said.

It was the longest conversation they'd had in days.

*　　*　　*

The first thing that caught your eye was the stained-glass window, oval and intricate, framed in white. The Virgin Mary, composed but perplexed, her hands clasped together in prayer for someone's soul—for hers, perhaps, and all the faithful departed.

Angel closed and locked her bedroom door, tossing the oversize purse onto her twin bed, kicking off her shoes, turning then toward her desk of antiqued white particleboard, the shelves overhead lined with teddy bears. They'd been collected for her since before she had a choice, and had felt they were such a waste of time, clenching her teeth into a tight smile as the collection grew with every birthday or Christmas. But now she treasured their every miserable stitch.

Lifting the largest of the group, sitting dead center on the highest shelf—Mr. Greenjeans, a fat beige teddy dressed in bib overalls and holding a small corncob pipe—Angel took him into her arms and brought him to her bed, taking a seat under the Virgin Mary.

From her bag she retrieved the cash given to her by Richard, counting the bills out as if therein lay the real pleasure. Then, unbuttoning Mr. Greenjeans's bib overalls, Angel gave a little tug to what should have been stitches on the bear's stomach. But the sound of Velcro gave her handiwork away. Reaching in, she removed first a handful of stuffing, cotton balls speckled with sawdust. Then, reaching in again, she pulled out a roll of bills as thick as her fist. All hundreds, crisp and new. Removing the rubber band that held the roll tight, she added Richard's donation to the stash. After wrapping it once again, she put it back into the teddy's tummy.

With the bear back in its place of honor, Angel flipped on her stereo. The beat grabbed hold, the number one song in the country this week. What else would she be listening to? She *pulled the little black dress from her bag and danced with it violently around her room, a partner made of silk who knew all the latest moves, before pulling back on a short bookcase, revealing the space—crawl space, storage space, hiding space—hidden behind it. She tossed the dress into the dark confines, kicking shut the bookcase door with the tips of her toes.*

Then, singing along, she got ready for bed, sliding off the jeans, her panties, and replacing the belly shirt with a long, oversize cotton T-shirt. Bare-assed and sassy, she danced her way into her bathroom, stopping at the sink, splashing water onto her face. Then, loading up her toothbrush with a minty gel, Angel brushed her teeth, moving the bristles in time with the tune, nodding her head to the beat as well, remembering suddenly her earliest life lesson, and how it so applied to Richard, and what he seemed to enjoy most about their encounters.

It made her giggle out loud and almost choke on the toothpaste.

Her mom's voice echoed in her head, always insisting Angel brush her teeth before going to bed.

Especially after a late-night snack.

Madison

It was louder than he expected.

Though Peter Robertson would have been the first to admit he didn't know what to expect.

The young actress who played Angel, stepping out from the wings now, standing in front of the set for her bedroom, three breakaway walls, no ceiling, the floor spilling out to the edge of the stage. She was bending at the waist to the applause, the cheers of "Bravo!" The delight on her face genuine as the first member of the audience stood, followed by another, then in a heart-beat, everyone standing, a bouquet of flowers in her arms, tears.

The members of the cast all joined hands now, the ac-tress playing Angel flanked on one side by the actor who played her father, and on the other by the actress who played her mother, the other cast members com-pleting the line, bowing in unison to the cheers.

The play's writer/director came out last: Sam Fried-man, a burly man with Einstein hair and a goofy grin, who'd been in Madison his entire life. He never saw a reason to leave; there were no greater aspirations filling his heart. He wasn't sure he'd ever want to, or that there ever would be. Madison was home. There was no life beyond Madison.

He pressed down the enthusiasm with both hands, then wiggled his fingers back up as if to encourage more. Laughing, wiping the nonexistent beads of sweat from his brow with a wave of his hand and an exaggerated "Whew!" He was a ham enjoying his moment in the spotlight.

"Normally at the Willy Street Playhouse," Sam began, "when we adapt a book or movie, about halfway into the run we get a cease-and-desist letter from some attorney."

A number of people in the small audience laughed as if they'd been on the receiving end of those letters. As if it were a rite of passage in the underground theater world, so far off-off-off-Broadway.

"That won't be the case this time," Sam said. "Peter Robertson, the author of *Angel*, the novel upon which this play is based, graciously granted me permission. Why?" Sam shrugged. "I don't know for certain, but I do think he deserves a round of applause." He pointed toward the center of the audience, four rows back, where Peter was sitting. "Peter, take a bow."

Most in the audience turned toward Peter then, a hushed gasp tossed his way, as if his presence were a miracle of Old Testament proportions, then suddenly the loudest cheers yet, erupting, forcing Peter to his feet.

At six-four he felt gawky and embarrassed as he gave the slightest of waves. He wasn't used to applause. Most writers weren't. He was used to sitting alone for six to eight hours a day, seven days a week, in front of a computer monitor, trying to make sense of, trying to make entertaining, the jumbled stories in his head. He was used to typing, and the comforts of home. Peter didn't get out much.

Turning toward his left, he caught the eye again of a young woman who'd been staring at him throughout, from when he first arrived at the small Madison, Wisconsin, theater and was greeted as if royalty by Sam and an older woman named Clara who ran the box office.

The young woman had been sitting outside by herself, on a bench near the ticket window, her fingers playing nervously with a loose thread on her sleeve. Peter wondered at the time if she were to pull on it, would her top come unwound and disappear? Or would she?

Petite, dressed entirely in black, she was a tragic Goth princess with eyes like a Margaret Keane nymph. Peter remembered catching her eye for the first time as he walked up the path that led to the theater. She had looked away then, suddenly, a small smile playing at the corners of her mouth. A small sigh escaping her crimson lips.

She watched him as well from her seat during intermission, as Peter sat quietly by himself, reading over the program, the short bios of the cast and crew, most of whom made their theatrical home at Willy Street. She'd look away or down whenever he raised his eyes, catching his glance only once, a quick bite-down on her bottom lip, eyes darting to the left, as if caught in a lie, or a heartbreak.

And now the young woman seemed to cheer the loudest, her eyes wide and appreciative, so endlessly green, set large in an oval-shaped face ringed by jet-black hair. She reminded him of an older Angel, the teenager molded by Rodin into a woman, the slightest of lines scratched by fingernails into the impressionable clay on the sides of her mouth as she smiled, the baby fat of her cheeks pressed into angles of radiance.

Or at least, that was how Peter would write her, how he was describing Angel now in the second book, the sequel, *It's a Wonderful Lie.* Angel at the ripe age of twenty-one.

He stared at her, bowing his head once in acknowledgment, and finally she refused the opportunity to turn away.

It was as if Angel had come to life and was giving her creator a round of applause.

Something about that frightened Peter.

Something about it inexplicably turned him on.

Other Plans

When the houselights came on, she was gone—her seat empty, not even a program rolled tightly, its corners turned, a piece from a back page torn to make a chewed-gum wrapper, littering the floor to give hope that she was really once there.

Peter watched the audience clear out. He listened to their hushed discussions of the story, the cast members, what was missing from the book, what was new and/or different. Stepping into the theater's cramped lobby, he found Sam shaking hands like a politician after a landslide victory.

The play's writer/director smiled, and shook Peter's hand as well. "Was it worth coming all the way out to Madison to see your words mangled by a hack like me?" he asked.

Peter knew it was a question he'd be asked. There was no getting around it. On the flight to Wisconsin he'd conjured up every possible response, depending on his opinion. If the play blew him away, it would be easy; his enthusiasm would show through. But being kind in the face of mediocrity—or worse, what if the play was bad to the point of being laughable?—that was the challenge.

He luckily found himself somewhere in between. Was it the greatest theater of all time? Not hardly. But it entertained for two hours and kept even him guessing as to the outcome, and he wrote the damn book. And it *was* fun to see his words come alive. He had always wanted to hear Angel's dialogue, see how she'd act or react. He had always wanted a flesh-and-bones Angel, real, even if only for two hours, even if only to shake her hand.

Though in the back of his mind, an old favorite cliché of his father's would ring through: *Be careful what you wish for.* Peter knew a *real* Angel would be a handful, trouble. Dangerous, even. He'd written her that way.

"Sam," Peter said, "it . . . was . . . therapeutic."

From the beaming grin on the director's face, *therapeutic* was good. "I just used the words you wrote," Sam said. "Everything I needed was right there on the page."

Peter nodded, turning away just slightly, the swinging pendulum of a beaten-down grandfather clock catching his eye. The gleam off the brass triggering the image. A shiny circle. It had been haunting him, playing in his mind. . . .

A hubcap lying flat on worn gray asphalt. Suddenly it starts to spin upward. Rising to its side, rolling back up the street in reverse motion.

Always backward, as if trying to get home.

He just wanted for it to stop, wanted for it to go away, but these images never went away completely when he was writing. He'd blink; they'd appear. Another blink, and they'd be gone. That seemed part of the process, living the words before they made it to the page. Fucked-up home movies playing on a seemingly endless loop in his head. His own creations haunting him every step of the way. This time backward.

Sam was talking again, a man who liked to talk, and Peter wondered why he hadn't become an actor instead, relishing every night the sound of his own voice.

"We're all headed to the Institute for a drink," he said. "You in?"

"Yeah, um, sure," Peter said, glad that his distraction wasn't obvious, thinking this was why writers should never be allowed beyond their front doors when working on a book. The real world held so little interest by comparison. "What else is there to do in Madison?" he joked.

"Not much," Sam replied. "Meet you outside in five."

Nodding, watching the director head back into the theater, Peter turned, taking in the play's poster. It was a different image, nothing like Angel's various book covers. A teenage girl was all that connected them. In this shot, her black hair wet, falling into her eyes, she looked at herself in a mirror, perhaps a little high, a little confused, her hand large in the foreground, touching the mirror, reaching out as if to save herself from falling through to the other side. The polish on her fingernails was delicately chipped, broken flakes of purple and black, as if from scratching away at her insides. Alice's damaged half sister in the looking glass. The word ANGEL sickly and bright, in a shaky font, as if written on the mirror by someone who'd been abused her entire life, and was now confined to a mental institution, told everything was her fault. *Based on the novel by Peter Robertson*, the same shaky hand had the single-minded tenacity to write. The R in Robertson was backward, like in the famous toy store logo. But this was no game.

"Excuse me, Mr. Robertson," came the voice, hoarse, low in register, a little shy, yet still sexy, as if born into a world of pain, a life spent hiding behind what pleasure her body might bring.

Peter turned and came face-to-face with her then, the young woman in black from the audience who cheered so enthusiastically as he stood. She was sublime up close, sharp-edged and radical. So unlike the others in Peter's life. So unlike him. He wished he could dress from head to toe in black, with boots made for stomping. But he'd feel . . .

"I feel like such a"—she shrugged, smiled, and admitted it finally—"*dork* asking this, but . . ."

Exactly, Peter thought, why he could never dress in black, watching her as she reached into her bag, a large black purse with twin straps studded with silver skulls, slung over her left shoulder: *I'd feel like a dork.*

He flinched back just slightly, as if expecting a gun or knife, or something that might do him harm. That dork reflex . . . who was he kidding? It was the book again, the words in his head, dealing with the violent life and death of his characters, and maybe Peter was expecting a little revenge. One could play God for only so long without repercussions. But would a killer ever use the word *dork*?

Not noticing, so blissfully unaware, the young woman pulled an old copy of *Angel* from the bag and held it out to Peter.

"A first edition," he said, laughing at his own paranoia. He took the book, turning it over in his hands, opening it to the copyright page. "Where'd you get this?"

"I've had it forever," she replied.

This was the *first* of *Angel*'s many covers, the *first* of its very many printings. A blurry photo of a young woman's face from the nose up. Her eyes were wide and smeared with mascara, her jet-black hair cut in a bob, with bangs straight over her eyebrows.

"There are only a thousand of these," Peter said, admiring the crispness of the binding, how tight the pages seemed, as if the book were not only never read, but just published, hot off the presses. "Publisher didn't think it would sell."

"Guess they were wrong," came the same shy voice.

"Always hated this cover, though," Peter added.

"No, no," the young woman protested, "the cover's perfect."

"Really?" He looked at her now, as she stared down at the book in his hands. Here was another mirror image, and he understood immediately her connection.

"I love the cover," she said.

He hadn't any doubt now, watching her as her hand ever so lightly brushed the face on the dust jacket.

"That's me," she said, looking up at him, smiling.

Her sincerity was intoxicating.

"For what it's worth," Peter said, "you're a lot prettier than she is."

But it was as if she didn't hear him, not responding, but continuing, "This book is me."

Peter forced a small smile as the young woman held out a pen.

"Could you, please?" she asked.

"Of course," Peter said.

"Make it out to Dina," she said.

"Dina," Peter repeated, liking the sound of her name.

"It means 'God has judged,'" she explained.

"Oh, really?" Peter replied, amused. He always looked up the meanings of his characters' names. But how many people in everyday life knew what their own names meant? Not many, he figured. His meant 'a rock.' Hardly fitting. "Is that an appropriate name for you, then?"

"I like to think so," she said.

Peter opened the book to the title page, pen poised. "Anything special you want me to write?" he asked.

Without hesitation, Dina replied, "You've already written it."

Peter smiled, a lot more sincerely this time, signing her book, then handing it back. He wished he could speak so easily and freely. But his words seemed to work only on the page.

"Thank you so much," she said, staring at his signature, beaming, before gently closing the book and returning it to her bag.

"Ready?" Sam's voice boomed from somewhere behind Peter's shoulder, loud and confident, the director, another rendition of *Action!*

Nodding. "Yeah, umm . . ." Peter very politely asked a question, which he would frequently recall later, wondering if there was anything flirtatious to his tone, his smile. "We're all going up the street for a drink. Care to join us?" he asked, adding, "I mean, if you don't have other plans."

She didn't.

Dina

He wouldn't shut up.

An actor, Tony Rialto, or Bialto, or something that sounded like a pre–Great Depression–era movie palace. Dina didn't care, wouldn't remember.

He had played Richard in the play. The lover, the married john, the one who first exposed Angel to luxurious new worlds when she answered his sugar-daddy ad in the *Village Voice: Generous gentleman seeking adventurous and discreet young women who desire the finer things in life.*

Angel was thirteen when she first answered the ad.

Fourteen when he first put a spoon up to her nose.

Rialto was talking about his craft, his training, the interest from Hollywood, and the number of Willy Street productions in which he'd appeared. He was quoting from a review in the *Belleville Gazette* that compared his intensity to Brando's.

"But I'm ready for more," Tony Rialto said.

Dina was thinking the exact same thing. She was seated at a large steel table, next to Peter, but back-to-back at the moment. Not touching, but close enough so that the warmth radiated hyperkinetic sparks, a high-speed wireless connection, encrypted and oh so private.

Most of the cast were there, and many who she imagined were members of the technical crew. The play's writer/director, Sam, was bending Peter's ear, talking nonstop, while Peter appeared to mumble nothing more than the occasional "Uh-huh," peppered with infrequent nods. And while Dina saw it as an opportunity to sip her drink in peace, and let the excitement of sitting so close take hold, Rialto saw it as time to move in for the kill.

She took in her surroundings, trying to tune the actor out. The place was called the Institute, a theme bar that would probably work only in the Midwest. The waitresses and bartenders were dressed as nurses and orderlies, with stethoscopes around their necks, listening to the heartbeats of their customers—anything for a tip. All was white and sterilized, like a nuthouse: padded walls, wheelless gurneys as tables, machines that went beep and ping, flatlining in time to the incessant throb of bass from some deejay who called himself the Doctor, pumping out bad eighties New Wave dance mixes like mood-altering pills. It was all so fifteen years ago.

Dina pulled the swizzle stick from her drink, noticing then that it was a scalpel made of silver plastic. She wished it were real, so she could cut out Rialto's heart and hand it to him on a silver plastic petri dish, allowing him the ultimate death scene, and putting everyone else out of their misery.

"Next stop for me, Broadway," Rialto said. "I'm moving to New York as soon as this run is over."

Never more bored in her twenty-one years on this planet, Dina sucked the Cointreau residue off the scalpel and said, "I couldn't imagine living anywhere else."

Perhaps it was fate, or that Sam was actually taking a breath between words, but it was quiet just for that moment, long enough, quiet enough, for Peter to hear.

He turned without hesitation. "You live in New York?" he asked.

Dina turned away from Rialto as he was in midsentence, something about all the agents clamoring for meetings the moment he arrived in the Big Apple. That was what Rialto called it, "the Big Apple," more out of step even than their surroundings.

Her eyes locked on Peter's, and she promised herself they weren't letting go.

"You came all the way out here to see the play?" he asked.

Dina smiled. She'd been thinking about how she'd explain it since purchasing the airline ticket, since pressing PURCHASE NOW on the online order form, a deeply discounted fare, but still, coming from New York just to see the opening of some play most people would never care about. She narrowed it down to either a compliment or a joke, figuring she'd decide on the spot.

She went with the joke.

"I did it for the miles," she said.

Peter laughed, sincerely. His smile was beautiful and strong, opening up dimples on the sides of his face, and laugh lines she so wanted to touch. She'd been thinking about that as well, touching him. A fantasy since . . . she was fifty-four pages into her first encounter with *Angel*, when she realized, closing the book for a moment to look again at Peter's photo on the back of the dust jacket. She'd read the book so many times since, countless times, often just opening to a random section to read for a few moments before going to sleep, thoughts of Peter in her head.

"What part of the city do you live in?" he asked.

"East Village, Alphabet City," she said.

"No way! Where?"

"Five Seventy-one East Sixth Street," she replied, adding hopefully, "if you must know."

"We're practically neighbors," he said.

"Where do you live?" she asked.

"East Tenth, between First and A," Peter said.

"I knew you lived downtown, but . . ."

Dina shrugged as a nurse, or waitress, or whatever the hell she was, put another round of drinks down in front of them.

"Thanks," Peter said, but he was looking at Dina, motioning with his chin down toward her drink. "Let me guess, a Cointreau on the rocks?"

"That was too easy," Dina replied. It was Angel's drink at the end of the book, the one vice she still allowed herself. It had no connection to her past.

"But I never take anything for granted," Peter said.

"You should," Dina replied, surprising herself with the suggestiveness of her tone. "Some things are certain."

Peter lifted his beer, taking a sip, looking away. She was pretty sure he had to.

Tony Rialto tapped Dina on the shoulder. "I was thinking that when I get to New York, maybe you and I could—"

She turned quickly, cutting him off with surgical accuracy. One look was all it took, a look only Rialto could see.

Normally a guy like Tony Rialto would have found such a reaction a turn-on, a challenge. Normally he'd have a comeback waiting, something just funny or charming enough to break the ice princess down. But there was something about Dina's scowl that instead made him stand immediately and move to another table.

Peter was watching her as she turned back. His smile caught her a little off guard. "So I guess this officially makes you my biggest fan," he said.

That surprised her, thrilled her, coming from Peter.

"*Angel* really is my favorite book," Dina said, unable to mask her devotion. She bit down on her bottom lip, her face angled downward just slightly as she looked up into Peter's eyes. "It's genius."

"Wow. Thank you," he said, "but . . . I, ah . . . y'know, I never for a moment thought that something I wrote could be anyone's favorite book."

He stared at her, waiting for a response. But Dina had nothing more she needed to say, at least, not at the moment. Right at the moment words seemed limiting in the pleasure they might give.

What she needed was for her and Peter to be alone.

Closing time. The cast and crew members talked in small groups on the sidewalk. Had Dina cared, she would have noticed that Tony Rialto was nowhere to be seen, having left the bar after an unnecessary bathroom run. Director Sam was bending Peter's ear once again. She watched as they talked, touching up her lipstick, wondering, How long before it came off?

"Thank you again," Sam said, shaking Peter's hand.

"It was my pleasure, Sam," Peter said. "Really."

Peter looked around then, as if ready to raise his arm to hail a taxicab. Dina followed his line of sight up and down the street, not dangerous, just dark. The two-story brick buildings and old Colonials fast asleep. Overgrown sidewalks, and old economy cars parked on both sides.

"You looking for a taxi?" Sam asked.

"Yeah," Peter said, "I'm pretty much out of luck, aren't I?"

The director seemed completely amused. "Damn New Yorkers," he said, then, "You need a ride back to your hotel?"

"Please," Peter said, then turning toward Dina, asked, "Where are you staying?"

"The Best Western across from the Capitol," she said, eliciting just the response she had hoped for.

Peter smiled, pleasantly surprised.

But it was Sam who spoke, waving the way toward an old Pontiac Sunbird.

"Then c'mon," he said. "It seems that I would be going your way."

Standing in front of the Best Western near a bank of newspaper boxes, Peter and Dina watched as the taillights on Sam's car faded away, a red highlight into the night.

It was chilly. No traffic, no people, no sounds. But still, Dina couldn't look at Peter for fear of what her expression might reveal. Instead she stared up at the gold dome of the state capitol, her hands together, as if in prayer. She needed strength.

"Want to come up for one more drink?" Peter asked.

"I don't know," she said, turning around then. "I think I'm already a little drunk."

Peter smiled.

Dina felt as if she suddenly could not breathe.

"So one more won't matter," he said, with what seemed to be a matter-of-fact shrug.

Dina stared at him for a beat, as if trying to read what was on his mind, as if trying to see if they could possibly want the same thing. Or was he just being friendly, just inviting her up to his room for a drink and nothing more?

"I think there's even some Cointreau in the minibar," he said, as if he needed to sell her on the idea.

Clenching her eyes shut, Dina sucked in a breath, the air clean, almost invigorating, like mint. Then she let it go, slowly, her breath whooshing out of her lungs, up her throat, and out her mouth. She smiled, opened her eyes, and looked at him then.

"Well, in that case," she said.

She hadn't come all the way out to Madison to just see a stupid play.

What We Wish For

"Green means go," Dina said.

They were standing in the hallway outside room 506. Peter was fumbling with the magnetic key card, sliding it into the slot, waiting for the red light to turn green, for the handle to give. On the third try, it did.

His room was sterile in most every way, antiseptically generic. Two twin-size beds, each covered with a floral bedspread. An individually wrapped thin mint resting precariously on each pillow. On the off-white-painted wall over each bed hung a reproduction of a landscape that never should have been painted to begin with, by a painter who should never have been allowed near a brush and palette. Thirty inches from the foot of the bed nearest the door, a nineteen-inch color TV hid inside an oversize armoire that doubled as a dresser and home for the minibar. At about the same distance from the second bed was a small table with two chairs pushed into the corner by the windows, which gave Peter a rather pleasant view of one of the two lakes on either side of downtown Madison. Which lake exactly, Mendota or Monona, he couldn't remember at the moment. He'd looked it up after checking in, but right now that seemed so long ago.

It had been a while since he'd been in a hotel alone— since he'd been anywhere alone, for even one night. A good fourteen or so years. Traveling alone had never been his idea of a good time. He liked having someone special with which to share the sights, the sounds, the humor of a situation. The bed. He liked having someone special to hold.

Opening the armoire, Peter bent at the knees, turning the key that kept the minibar locked, a key that he had found in place, in the flimsy lock to the door of what was nothing more than a dorm room fridge, as if booze here were on an honor system, and there could never be crime in a place like Madison. Any drunk who visited would respect that.

A puff of frozen air escaped, as if vapor locked inside. The fridge was stocked with overpriced bags of almonds and tubular cans of processed potato chips with red plastic resealable suction lids, as well as bottled water, cans of most every variety of soda, three bottles each of imported, domestic, and domestic light beers, and a door filled with miniature one-shot bottles of top-shelf booze.

Calculating in his head that he was about to spend twenty dollars on what was most likely skunky beer and a drink he had to prepare himself, Peter grabbed the import and a tiny bottle of Cointreau, along with a tray of ice cubes from the small compartment masquerading as a freezer. Concentrating on the task, he unwrapped the second of the two glasses that came with the room, the first already having been used as a toothbrush holder, and filled it with a handful of ice.

Returning the tray first to the freezer before twisting off the top of the bottle and dumping the tangy contents over the ice, he then twisted off the top of his beer and, with both drinks in hand, turned toward Dina.

She was sitting on the bed closest to the windows, leaning back on her elbows, her legs dangling off the end, knees just far enough apart. She was watching him. Peter knew she'd never taken her eyes off him as he prepared the drinks. He could feel her gaze, and he wondered now if perhaps he'd been a little too friendly. Whether a nightcap carried with it certain expectations, implied and expected to be rendered.

"Are you working on another book?" she asked as he walked toward her.

Harmless enough, he thought, nodding, handing her the glass of Cointreau. "The sequel," he said, taking a seat on one of the chairs surrounding the table, the chair facing the edge of that second bed straight on.

Dina looked confused.

"*It's a Wonderful Lie*," Peter explained. "Or at least, that's the working title." He shrugged. "I felt there was more to Angel's story. That I wasn't ready to let her go."

Dina took a long sip of her drink. "Aren't you afraid?" she asked, her tone dropping some of its flirtatious melody.

"Of what?"

"That you'll"—she shrugged—"make a mistake?"

"A mistake?"

"And she won't seem as real anymore."

Peter shook his head. He had given this a lot of consideration. Could a second book ruin the impact of the first? Absolutely, he'd seen it done so many times. But he wouldn't let that happen with Angel. He'd taken his time with this one. Years. The first book had afforded him that luxury. He'd given his character room to grow, mature, get angry. Learn from her mistakes.

"No, she's my creation—"

Dina cut him off. "But in the hearts and minds of your readers, Angel is—" she began passionately.

Peter returned the favor, cutting her off as well. ". . . a fictional character."

She turned away from him, looking over toward the door. Peter figured she was ready to go, as if suddenly disappointed, as if whatever little fantasy she might have had playing in her head had better remain a fantasy. He wondered if Dina's father had ever warned her to be careful what she wished for.

She finished off her drink, but made no move to leave. Instead she said, "I'll have another. If you don't mind."

Watching her, nodding to himself, Peter stood and returned to the fridge. As he leaned into the minibar for a second bottle of Cointreau, Dina asked, "How come your wife didn't come out for the premiere?"

The line was paraphrased right out of his first book, exactly as he'd always imagined Angel saying it. *Playing the wife card* was how Angel referred to it. The ace of spades when the married man pissed you off. The married man who was playing single, a bachelor with the luck to have lured a girl like Angel home. When she was paid enough she played along.

Peter returned to his seat, leaning forward, unscrewing the cap, dumping the contents of the small bottle into the glass Dina held flat on the bed by her hip.

"You are married, right?" she asked. "Twelve years. Your wife's name is Julianna. She's an assistant DA.

You have a little girl named Kimberly. A yellow Lab named Groucho."

Peter froze, staring at her, suddenly wanting her out of his room. Suddenly wishing they'd never met, never spoken, beyond him signing her book. What could he have been thinking?

"How do you know all that?" he asked.

"Your Web site, Peter," she said. "It's all there for anyone to memorize."

He sat back in the chair then, feeling no relief. Why would anyone want to memorize it? he wondered.

"What?" she said, laughing suddenly, leaning forward, resting her elbows on her knees. "Are you worried I'm some obsessed fan?"

No Regrets

Dina never gave Peter the chance to answer. She finished her drink quickly, then stood, placed the glass firmly on the table near his left elbow, and said, "It's getting late."

Agreeing, Peter followed her toward the door, opening it for her, looking down the hallway and back, as if expecting to be caught with a guilty conscience, his wife and daughter making a surprise visit.

"Want me to walk you to your room?" he asked politely—ever the Boy Scout, opening doors, helping old women across the street, offering obsessed fans a safe escort to their hotel rooms in the middle of the night. He stepped back into the room, leaning flat against the wall so she could pass without coming too close.

No such luck.

Dina smiled. "Why?" she asked, stopping in front of him. "Is there something we can do there that we can't do here?"

"I, ah . . . I'm not sure how to answer that question," Peter said, realizing he'd never have had the guts to ask it in the first place.

She laughed—it was sexy and a little drunken—then put a hand flat against his chest, drumming her fingers against him in time to a song he'd never hear.

"I can't tell you what an honor it was to meet you. To get to talk with you," she said, looking up into his eyes, moving incomprehensibly closer. "I was so scared about approaching you."

Peter just wanted for her to stop talking and leave. He could feel the fluster—or was it the alcohol, too many damn drinks? What was he thinking?

"You should . . . live your life with no regrets," he said, not able to explain the words coming out of his mouth. "I would never have written one word if I were afraid."

Christ, he thought, *I live every day frightened of losing what's mine.*

"Really?" she asked. "You just went for it?"

"Absolutely," he said, another lie. It took years to muster the courage to start a book.

Nodding, as if she agreed completely, or at least understood, Dina leaned up on her toes to kiss Peter on the mouth.

He moved his head away at first, a breath of exasperation, a car wreck of immediate guilt. But turning back, his mouth greeted hers furiously. It wasn't what he wanted, but instead what he needed more than his feeble words could ever express.

"I don't know if this is such a good idea," he said finally and, later he would admit, much too late.

Dina's hands moved from Peter's chest down over his stomach, lower, past the buckle of his belt, feeling him harden, rubbing him harder through his pants. He wanted to break her open.

"Sure it is," she said as she lowered his zipper, leaning up to kiss him again and to whisper into his ear, "I want to know what you taste like."

Another line he'd written for Angel to say. One of her clinchers, making her worth the price. His character in the here and now, and . . .

"No," he said, "really."

Dina shushed him, then dropped to her knees, staring up into his eyes all the while, exactly as he knew she would, no matter how much he protested otherwise.

He'd written Dina the most explicit instructions. Every fantasy since his first hard-on, collected, revisited, and revised in that first book. Every line he'd wanted a woman to speak to him. Every word he wanted to answer back, but never could—there in his fiction.

No one knew, not for sure. Not even his wife, Julianna. It was just a book, part of his warped imagination. It wasn't supposed to be an autobiography of his fantasies. But what else was there to a work of fiction besides the person the author could never be?

Her mouth was so warm, her grip so tight, her tongue like a kaleidoscope. And those eyes, holding fast and hard on to his. She was his Lolita. His Juliet. His *Girl with a Pearl Earring*.

His creation, more than any actress could ever hope to be.

It took no time for Peter to finish, his head pressed back against the wall, his eyes clenched tight, his breathing ragged and desperate. He was frightened, thinking that what was in his head should stay in his head. Or on a page.

Standing, her smile reflecting a sexy confidence, Dina put him away, like returning a treasured toy to the toy box, zipping his pants back up, none the wiser.

"I wasn't nearly as scared about doing that," she said before turning, walking through the doorway, and disappearing down the Best Western hallway.

His breathing still heavy, his mind now a turbulent storm, Peter wanted to say something, to react as a character in his novel might. To follow, to shrug it off, to say something, dammit.

But where was the response he'd penned for himself? Had all the good dialogue gone to Angel? Had he relegated himself to a supporting role, just another of her willing victims?

No immediate answers came to mind.

Homesick

Rocking himself wretched on the American Airlines flight bound for LaGuardia, Peter leaned forward, then back, repeating the motion in his aisle coach seat, wondering not about what he had done, but why. How could he have allowed it to happen?

"It was a mistake," he kept whispering to himself, his row empty, no one to feed on his paranoia, on his guilt. No one to wonder if he might be a threat to national security.

And there was no one to blame but himself.

He had drunk too much—*drunk*, great excuse, falling for her compliments, for that look in her eyes. The brushes against him at the bar, the way her shoulder pressed against his, not for a lack of space, but because she wanted to be touching him. He wanted her touching him. He had pressed back against her instead of moving away.

How long had it been since he'd noticed a woman looking at him that way? A stranger wanting him that way? Saying all the right things? Hitting all the right buttons, in the right order? Right because he had written them for her. She had explicit instructions.

He was sure no one would ever find out. That he and his wife would never run into Dina while picking up groceries, or at the movies on a Saturday night, or at their favorite restaurant.

But if they did . . . what could she possibly say? "Your husband told me all about you while I was giving him head in his hotel room." The thought made him nauseous.

Psycho women were mostly a figment of soap opera–fed imaginations. The fatal attractions made for guilty pleasures and good reading. They kept the viewers and readers coming back. Dina was just a fan living out a fantasy. She probably followed all of her favorite authors around, a writers' groupie. But instead of plaster casts of genitalia, she collected just memories and autographs.

Hopefully nothing more than memories and autographs.

Peter sighed, thinking he'd probably never see Dina again. Pressing his head back against the headrest, looking first up—the numbers of the row across the way, written in reverse: FED 22—then down, around, catching first a glimpse of the in-flight movie on the small monitor overhead—the old Christmas standby starring Jimmy Stewart, though Christmas was months away—then two thirty-something blond stewardesses with Botoxed foreheads preparing the drink cart, then . . .

"Christ!" he muttered, leaning forward suddenly for a better look.

A few rows up and across the aisle. The black hair,

the Gothic attire. And small hands holding high a trade paperback novel with a cover made to attract damaged young women.

It was as if he couldn't control the urge. Perhaps he'd lost all control—*I couldn't help myself*, an even better excuse. Standing, catching the headrest on the seat across the aisle for balance, he made his way toward her. Suddenly he wanted to see her, to say something about what happened last night. That it never should have. Or perhaps that it was wonderful.

"What a surprise," he said.

She looked up from her book, confused, but not alarmed. She actually smiled slightly.

"Excuse me?" she said.

She was younger. And Dina might at one time have seemed so innocent. Perhaps in the womb.

"I'm sorry," Peter said, suddenly disappointed, at a loss for words. "I thought you were . . ." How to finish the sentence? he wondered. *From the side you looked just like a girl who . . .*

Shaking his head instead, "Sorry," turning away, walking onward, pressing into the first lavatory marked UNOCCUPIED.

Latching the door behind him, the light going on, leaning over just in time, he threw up into the toilet, as if guilt had taken on form. His guts, his lungs, he might as well have spit out his heart.

Straightening up, but on shaky legs, he splashed water onto his face from the tiny sink, looking at himself then in the mirror. It was as if he'd aged years in Madison. As if violating a sacred vow had scratched a decade from his life. Infidelity should come with a warning label.

He could feel it coming on again, like a blackout, as the lights collapsed.

The visions, the antagonized inspiration, little snippets of films playing on a creaky projector, scratched and dirty, the sound track popping, sprocket holes torn, making the image jumpy, a little out of focus, projected on a dirty sheet in some back room of his mind. His personal smut. The night dank, the heat oppressive. Perhaps he was envisioning hell.

Peter gripped the edge of the sink, wondering if these were a blessing or a curse, a necessity to write, because either way, he just wanted them to go away, to push them away, back from wherever they came. He could live without ever writing another word if they would just go away.

The hubcap rolling backward up the street, flashing silver and grime, bouncing up onto a car wheel, which stopped suddenly, no choice in the matter, or perhaps all the choice in the world. Crashing like a 747, the images that haunted New Yorkers all too well, but here at street level. Here. Loud. Panicked screeches.

Peter caught his breath like a fastball slapping into his chest. He splashed more water onto his face, thinking that maybe he wasn't strong enough for this. That he couldn't handle betrayal.

That he couldn't control the characters in his head.

What Girls Like

The calls of "Daddy, Daddy!" rang out through the terminal. The light, slapping footsteps against linoleum, running, joyous in their rhythm and bounce.

Peter looked up through the dread that enveloped him like amniotic fluid to see her running his way. He wasn't sure at first if it was all in his head. The characters playing tricks on him. Fucking with his mind. Making the moment light. Allowing him a respite from the pain.

Then she called out, "Daddy," again.

And Peter smiled.

He would have smiled if he knew his next breath would be his last. Such was how happy she made him, how proud. He bent at the knee, scooping up into his arms the little girl with the long straight hair, dirty blond and fine. Giving her a mighty hug as he stood and spun her around, making her laugh.

Her name was Kimberly.

"Hey, pumpkin!" he said, kissing her cheek. He'd called her that since the day she was born, her face puffy and round. And sure, deep down he knew justborns were hardly beautiful, but she was the most beautiful thing he'd ever seen.

Second-most beautiful.

Coming up right behind her, Julianna, whose crinkly, crooked smile was what made it all worthwhile. There were no mysteries to Peter as to life, or why any of us were here. Those were the simple questions. And he'd found his answer in a tall, long-legged, long-haired beauty.

His wife leaned up and gave Peter a kiss over their daughter's shoulder.

"What are you two doing here?" he asked, catching the eye of a man walking past, the look of disgust, as if this stranger knew of his deceit.

"Thought we'd surprise you," Julianna said.

He'd hardly been gone any time at all, and yet her voice seemed distant, mysterious, almost foreign. Perhaps it was the guilt. Or that they never should have been apart to begin with.

"It is a surprise," he said, smiling with a tight jaw, his own muscles working against him. "A nice surprise."

"A little personal limo service," Julianna said flirtatiously.

"How personal?" he asked.

She smiled, making a sexy growl in her throat.

"Mommy," Kimberly said in an annoyed, singsongy voice, making them both laugh, because they knew what was coming next, that though only six she was already embarrassed by her parents. "People can hear you."

They walked through the strangely deserted top floor of the short-term parking lot, toward the corner farthest from the elevator, as if every other space had been filled when the car had been parked. Heading toward the old Saab 900, mostly red, a little rusted, bought before the remodel, back when the car still looked like a cartoon turtle, back when it still held a certain charm.

Julianna tossed Peter the keys so he could open the back door and release Groucho, whose tail was wagging like the whip of a dominatrix during a seizure. The yellow Lab was happy to see him and could barely control his enthusiasm, jumping up, then down again, panting, running in circles. Pressing up finally against Peter's legs as Peter knelt to pet him.

"Hey, Groucho," he said. "How you doin', boy? You miss your dad?"

The dog whined and made a monkeyish sort of sound, his tail seeming to control his hindquarters now, shaking the Lab from the bottom up.

Peter laughed, so happy to see them all, so happy to know that even if Groucho knew what had transpired in Madison, he forgave his master, or at least overlooked it. A true best friend. Of course, he wasn't the one betrayed.

Peter looked up and caught Julianna watching him. "I'll take that as a yes," he said.

"You just give him more treats than I do," she said.

Popping the trunk, Peter lifted his suitcase, placing it gently inside, bending in, his back to his family, tugging on a zipper, retrieving a surprise. Then, standing, he turned toward Kimberly.

"Did you bring me a surprise?" she asked.

"What do you think?"

"Yes," she said. "What is it?"

"Well, close your eyes," he said, "and you'll find out."

"Daddy," she said impatiently, making a face. But still, she closed her eyes.

Flashing Julianna a goofy raised eyebrow, Peter pulled what looked to be an oversize triangle of yellow cheese from behind his back. It was really nothing more than a slab of foam, a cheesehead, as Green Bay Packer fans called them, dyed yellow, with a head-size cutout. He placed the souvenir on his daughter's head.

Julianna shot him a look as if to say he was completely nuts. "Nice," she said, not really meaning it, but seemingly amused nonetheless.

Snapping open her eyes, Kimberly took off the cheesehead to take a better look.

"Cool!" she said, the word exploding from her mouth as she turned the foam over in her hands before returning it to her head. She looked up at her dad with appreciative eyes. "It's, like, the coolest thing ever!"

Peter held the door open for her so that she and Groucho could hop into the backseat.

"See," he said to his wife.

Shaking her head just slightly, Julianna gave Peter another kiss, this one slightly more lingering, then said, "You always know what girls want."

"Umm," he said, lost in the kiss, handing her back her keys.

"Uh-uh," she said, instead opening the passenger-side door.

"What happened to the personal service?" he asked.

"That'll come later," she said, hinting at more than a ride home.

Peter pursed his lips.

She laughed.

"Right now," Julianna said, "it's rush hour on the LIE."

The Actress Who
Played Angel

Plain and simple, it sucked.

To hit speeds of ten miles per hour while driving the Long Island Expressway at rush hour seemed a miracle. Most of the time you just inched forward.

Peter gripped the steering wheel perhaps a little harder than necessary. Driving always made him tense. It was one of the reasons he chose to live in New York City: He rarely needed to get behind the wheel. Only on rare occasions, a quick trip to the Upper West Side health food store Julianna so loved, a trek into Jersey to pick up something for the apartment at IKEA. Once they all drove up to Boston to see a Mets game. But normally the Saab remained parked in space 258 in a garage half a block down from the building in which they lived.

"So, how was it?" Julianna asked.

"Hmm?" he said, turning to look at her, not knowing exactly what she was referring to, but the guilt suddenly making an encore. The guilt was a living, breathing entity. It was aware.

"Madison?" she said. "The play."

"Oh, right, um . . . it was strange, mostly," he lied. "I guess I never imagined *Angel* as a play."

"Just a blockbuster movie, right?" she said.

"Right," he said, "starring Julia Roberts."

It *had* been suggested. A deal had almost been in place, until the producers buying the rights to Peter's book made the mistake of telling him they were planning on making his character a little older—thirty, not in her mid-teens. Instead of a high school student, she'd be a divorced mother of two who prostituted herself to pay the bills, but who lost custody of her children when she became addicted to heroin. Her struggle would have been the fight to get straight and get her kids back. Julia Roberts was going to star, they told him. It was a long-overdue sequel of sorts to *Pretty Woman.* Peter thanked them for their time, then moments after ending the conference call, told his agent, Mike Levine, to take the book off the market. He would never need the money that badly.

"The girl who played Angel was great," he said.

"Like you pictured?" Julianna asked.

Peter thought for a moment, picturing not the actress, but Dina as she held out her first-edition *Angel* for him to sign. That ethereal glow on her face.

Perhaps she knew what would happen all along.

Maybe it was just admiration.

"Yeah," he answered quietly. "Exactly as I pictured."

"Was she nice?"

"Oh, um . . . I never really spoke to her," Peter said. Then, turning to look at his wife, turning to see if she could somehow measure his guilt, see it sitting on his shoulder like a drug monkey, flinging its own shit down into the hole in which Peter's soul once thrived, he asked, "Why?"

"I don't know," Julianna said. "In the back of my head I just always worried about you having an affair with the actress who brought Angel to life."

"Julia Roberts?" he asked, trying to make light of a situation of which only he was aware. He and Dina.

"Okay, maybe not with Julia Roberts," she replied. "But, y'know . . . there's your character in the flesh and blood. Speaking lines you wrote. Acting out, well . . . love scenes you . . ."

"Wrote," he suggested.

She shrugged. "How could you resist?"

"I can't believe you worry about me having affairs," he said—truthfully, but realizing sadly that she knew him better than he knew himself.

"Only when I'm bored," she said, reaching over and just touching lightly the side of his face. A *therapeutic* touch. Such a useful word. "And I've been very bored while you were away."

"We'll have do something about that," he said.

"You've got a lot of catching up to do, Peter Robertson."

Such truth, he thought. Then, turning to face her, Peter noticed the sudden widening of her eyes.

"Looks like it'll be sooner rather than later," she said.

Confused, he followed her point of view, turning to look out the windshield.

"About time," he said, breathing a sigh of relief.

The traffic had finally begun to move.

This particular traffic jam was over.

Home

He almost missed the street.

A tree-lined block of five- and six-story brownstones. A few off-kilter shops inhabiting the first floors or basements—a vintage clothing store, a guitar shop, another that sold nothing but used CDs, all East Village–appropriate, but otherwise nothing but apartments, some rent-controlled, many converted to overpriced condos. A one-bedroom that rented for 250 dollars a month back in the mid-seventies, selling for upward of a million dollars now. Or more.

East Tenth Street, between Avenue A and First Avenue. The East Village, once home to starving artists and heroin addicts, now gentrified, homogenized, sanitized. Home to rich artists and Adderall junkies.

The building was whitewashed brick, six stories, with a larger-than-usual front porch raised a half story high, with a passage underneath to the basement apartments below. The door was oak, solid except for an oval window with beveled edges. Passing through it you arrived in the foyer, a collection of twenty-four mailboxes, four one-bedroom condos each on the first five floors, another two in the basement, plus two three-bedroom units on the top floor. From there you could be buzzed in via intercom through a matching oak door, a twin.

Peter walked through the door now with his family. Claustrophobia was taking hold, not so much as if he couldn't breathe, but more likely that he didn't deserve to. That he had soiled the sanctity, corrupted the safety, left the doors wide-open for the horrors of the night.

Groucho took the lead, rushing through the pale green hallway, past apartments 1-A and 1-D, coming to a stop in front of the olive green elevator door, sitting, waiting. Kimberly pressed the call button. Julianna leaned her head back against her husband's shoulder.

He wanted to tell her. He wanted to be honest. There had never been lies between them. Never. He had never betrayed her; it was never even an issue. Then why this time? How could it have happened so quickly, so easily? How could it have happened at all?

The elevator dinged. The door slid open, revealing the mirrored back wall of the car. Peter caught a glimpse as they entered, as Kimberly pressed the button marked 6.

The family in the mirror, he thought, looked happy.

The door opened into the kitchen, small but functional, with a new fridge and an ancient stove whose pilot light had a borderline personality disorder. The countertops were a burnt-orange Formica from the early eighties. They were ugly when Peter and Julianna purchased the condo eight years back, when the New York real estate market was in a slump—they could never afford it today. They were just as ugly now, though part of their home's landscape. The flaw they grew not to love exactly, but to relish. ·

The kitchen cabinets were real wood with old-fashioned hinges on the door. One of the drawers stuck. Peter always seemed to forget which until it was too late, and his light tug on the handle threw him off balance. Their toaster was a wedding present, the only one that still worked, or was in one piece, or hadn't been thrown away. The farthest corner of the room was Groucho's space, his bowls side by side on the floor, both off-white ceramic with small dog bones dotting them like a dalmatian's spots: one for water, one for food.

The kitchen gave way to what they both called the living room. It was where they ate, watched TV, read. The largest room in the apartment, white walled, dotted with framed photos, artwork, knickknacks, with windows looking east, over the rooftops of the two closest buildings, both five stories tall. The dining room table had been a hand-me-down from Julianna's parents. Old oak, scarred by ten thousand meals, with matching chairs—matching except for the leg of one, which had been chewed on by Groucho when they first rescued him, a bored dog who didn't know any better. The sofa was dark green, worn, comfortable, flaked with dog hair no matter how many times Julianna vacuumed it. The end table and the coffee table were large and functional, covered with books and magazines and a collection of remote controls that no one completely understood, but still they'd somehow figure out how to turn on the TV, the stereo, the DVD, the VCR, and the cable box.

It was the room in which they really *lived*.

Peter placed his suitcase down alongside the sofa

and looked about the room. It seemed strangely unfamiliar, a distant memory shrouded in heavy fog.

Moving through the room, down the narrow hallway that led to the bathroom, their bedrooms, and . . .

Stopping in front of the door to his office, closed, an old brass knocker screwed in at eye level, the words *"Dieu et mon droit"* etched in under a lion and a horse facing each other, grappling over a heart. Over their heads hung a banner, and the date 1953. It was a memento from his grandfather's apartment, and Peter had not a clue as to what the knocker represented. The old man died before he could ask.

Turning the handle, he let the door swing open. It stopped midway, as it always had, the hinges stiff and creaking.

He stepped inside, thinking that anyone in that Madison audience would automatically make the connection. This was Angel's bedroom. The shelves were the same, just lined with books instead of teddy bears. And more important, there was the oval-shaped stained-glass window with the likeness of the Virgin Mary on the glass.

But looking around, Peter had difficulty connecting. Even in his office he felt uneasy, as if the tryst with Dina had made him a stranger in the place he called home.

He lifted an old set of handcuffs from his desk. They were now a paperweight, a toy, something to keep his fingers occupied when they weren't tapping the keyboard of his computer. Originally he had bought them so he could understand the games Angel played with her clients. And later her imprisonment. So he could better describe the sound, the feel. The power they held. The fear they could generate.

Opening and closing one of the cuffs now with one hand, pressing it through, the sharp clicks, then back over again. Peter checked through the messages and the mail they had held down, that they had imprisoned.

The calls were what he expected: his agent, his editor, a few old friends whom he rarely saw or spoke to anymore. The mail was mostly bills, some magazines, catalogs from Pottery Barn and Victoria's Secret, and offers of credit cards with zero interest.

Peter placed the handcuffs gently atop a two-and-a-half-inch-thick stack of pages. Ninety-five thousand words. The manuscript to *It's a Wonderful Lie*, which waited patiently on one corner of the desk for his return. Waited for him to finish, to set it free. Then he retrieved an old stiletto from a Mets mug that otherwise held pencils and pens. The knife was something he had bought at a pawnshop so long ago he could barely remember. Before he'd ever met Julianna. It was silver, with a nine-inch blade, the handle tarnished, with worn-down decorative swirls and his initials, which he'd had engraved so he could feel as if he'd owned it forever. He used it now as a letter opener. Back then he didn't use it at all.

Slicing open one of the pieces of mail, he removed the letter from the official-looking envelope, beige linen with a very serious font, and glanced over it. A goddamn bill. Past due—how had he forgotten? Where was his mind?

It was the last thing he needed right now, after what happened in Madison.

It angered him.

It made him sad.

Shaking his head, he returned the letter to the envelope, then shuffled it back into the stack, tearing it from his mind. Removing it, forgetting it, leaving a credit card application atop the pile for the time being.

There was too much clutter already—in his mind, in his life, in this room. The office was such a chaotic collection of trinkets and scraps of paper, notes randomly scribbled for the last book, for this one, for the ones in the future. The hidden storage space behind one of the lower cabinets, built by a previous tenant, he assumed, like the secret passageway from an old haunted mansion, crammed with boxes of revisions and tax returns a decade old. There was his collection of books lining the floor-to-ceiling shelves. A copy of every book Peter had ever read. Copies of books he planned to get to shortly. Copies of every printed version of *Angel*, the paperback, the French, the German, the Japanese editions.

Peter looked over at the shelf, chosen for copies of his own work because it was at his exact eye level, right there when he opened the door. He pulled from it a first-edition copy of *Angel*, Dina's edition.

Thumbing through the pages, he glanced at the dedication: *For Julianna and Kimberly*. And at the acknowledgments page, so short, so incomplete, so many goddamn names missing.

The guilty preferred to remain anonymous.

Now he understood why.

Jeffrey Halliwell

He felt so much younger back then.

What was it, four years ago? It seemed longer, or perhaps just yesterday. He'd finally been ready to make the leap from reporting on the ease with which so many people in this city could kill. The ease with which so many people had died on that one day in September 2001. Maybe that was the wake-up call. The frozen tears of countless thousands raining down upon his complacency. Maybe something in him had died that day as well, had been reborn. He'd written a few short stories over the years, in between the violence and sacrilege he covered on a daily basis for The New York Times. *Got them published even, in places where they'd be read. One was read by his agent, Mike Levine, who on their first meeting asked, "Are you working on a novel?"*

A novel? That was the dream, but . . . who had the time? And what would it take, six months, a year? They had enough money saved. Julianna's job was secure. Just the money they'd save alone on Kimberly's day care . . .

He took the plunge.

At her urging.

"I don't want you to ever look back and say, 'What if?'" Julianna told him at the time.

He didn't want to look back and say that either.

The research was harder than he expected. More emotionally draining.

The cops he befriended were detached and weary, the teenage prostitutes tarnished beyond repair. Their battle wounds cut deep; their slurred diction was hard on the ear. The drug dealers and pimps were a lot scarier than their prototypes on TV. Appalling and angry. Their guns a lot scarier in person.

Fear had a smell. Sex had a price. Death was a side effect.

And Peter was right back where he began.

He met Jeffrey Halliwell on a cold March afternoon. The sky was a clear, crisp blue. It was windy, the gusts fighting him at every step, burning through his coat, trying to keep Peter away from Halliwell's three-story West Village town house.

Perhaps the wind could see into the future.

"Don't be too impressed," Mike Levine had advised. "The crib's inherited."

But still, Peter thought, standing before a black oak front door through which Andre the Giant could pass, pressing the doorbell, the sound ringing through the neighborhood like the bells of Notre Dame. More intimidating than impressive.

Halliwell was a few years younger than Peter. He wore a black suit that flowed from his lean frame like silk hung from the guitar string of Les Paul. His watch, which he checked often, was worth more than what Peter would *normally earn in six months at the* Times. *His home was decorated from the ads of that same paper. Peter and Julianna had always wondered aloud who bought that furniture, the twelve-thousand-dollar Italian leather sectional sofa displayed on the back cover of the* Times' *TV guide. Now he knew.*

Peter also now knew that the sofa wasn't any more comfortable than their four-hundred-dollar Swedish special. If anything it seemed a little stiff, void of personality. Much like Halliwell himself, who sat across from Peter now, an expanse of smoked glass, the coffee table, with a bronze nude woman as its base, separating them.

Halliwell wrote down a number from memory on a slip of paper ripped from a leather notebook.

"His name's Raoul Santiago," Halliwell said, leaning forward, handing Peter the cheat sheet.

"Will he know what this is about?" Peter asked.

"He'll be expecting your call," Halliwell explained. "He can pretty much supply you with anything you need."

"I just need information," Peter said.

"He's got the best drugs," Halliwell said, as if he hadn't heard him, or wasn't listening, staring at Peter as he spoke, as if trying to decipher his motives. "Guns and girls." The left side of his mouth turned up in a sickening smile. "He's got 'em young, too, real fresh, if you're into that. Or just curious."

"I need information," Peter repeated, "that's all." He so wanted to get out of there, to move on—

—to lunge forward and strangle the life from Halliwell, who only snorted out a small laugh, looking away with disinterest, with amused disgust, as if Peter were far beneath him, not even worth a smirk.

Peter would remember the look; he'd describe it in the

book, but more important, he'd capture the way it made Angel feel. He knew the way it made Angel feel.

Or at least, how he thought it made Angel feel.

"Yeah," Halliwell said finally, standing dismissively. "So Mike said."

Takeout

"I was thinking of ordering takeout."

Julianna's voice came from the doorway to his office. Peter could picture the way she leaned her shoulder against the jamb, half in, half out. The curve of her body, where he'd place his hand on her hip if he were to kiss her right now.

She sounded a little tired tonight as she added, "Chinese?" a question, to see if he might be in the mood.

Seated at his desk, in the chair he had purchased when he first decided to give this book thing a shot—designed by a Czechoslovakian chiropractor to eliminate tension in the back—Peter nodded without turning around. Looking at her was so difficult right now.

"That works," he said, always in the mood for Chinese. Chinese and pizza. Mindless food, because food was usually the farthest thing from his mind when he was in work mode, and though only home for a few hours, he had already opened the WordPerfect file for *It's a Wonderful Lie* to start the rewrite immediately, as if it couldn't wait one more day. As if this rewrite would purge his soul.

"You gonna tell Daddy what Uncle Mike had to say?" Kimberly said. Her voice singsongy, all tattletale.

Peter tensed up. He turned then, looked up at his wife, standing as he imagined, his daughter leaning up against her mother's leg.

"Mike was here?" he asked, as if he himself were suddenly betrayed.

Julianna nodded. "Yes," she said, the fingers of one hand combing through Kimberly's hair in soothing repetition. "He wanted to know the truth about how the new book was going."

Remembering the visit made the little girl laugh. "He said he was gonna give you a spanking, Daddy," Kimberly said, "if you didn't finish your new book soon."

Still staring at his wife, Peter stood, going to Kimberly, suddenly dropping to one knee in front of her, playfully tickling her sides.

"The only one who's gonna get a spanking around here is Cheesehead," he said in a cartoonish voice.

"Uh-uh." She giggled.

"Now go wash up for dinner," Peter said. "We're getting Chinese."

A high-pitched "Yea" reverberated through the apartment as Kimberly ran from the office, down the hallway toward the bathroom, her arms spread wide as if she could fly like an airplane, or an angel.

"He couldn't just ask me?" Peter said, his tone a lot more understanding than what he was feeling inside. He was feeling rage, and he wasn't completely sure why.

"Honey," Julianna said, reaching for his hand, soothing it with a slight squeeze, "he's just worried because he hasn't seen any pages." She touched his face with her free hand. "None of us have."

Peter pointed at a stack of paper, a ream thick, sitting on the far left corner of his desk. The handcuffs holding down the title page, the link of the chain connecting the two cuffs appearing to be hooked on the word *lie*.

"The pages are right there," he said.

"And usually Mike would have read them by now," she said. "He read every draft of the first book, Peter. We both did." She shook her head. "I haven't read one word from you in almost a year."

Every word he wrote was for her.

"You can't read this now," he said realistically. "You don't have the time."

She nodded. A sad truth. Work, life in general. When was there ever enough time?

"He asked me if you were happy," she said.

Peter shook his head, mouthing the word *happy* as a question.

"With the job he's done for you," she explained.

"What are you talking about?"

"Mike thinks you're talking to other agents, that you're ready to move on," she said.

"But that's"—he shook his head, feeling confused now, the emotion showing in his tone—"ridiculous. It makes no sense."

"I know," she said. "I told him that . . . but *Angel* sold well."

"That's no guarantee the next one will."

"He's afraid you'll be moving on to a bigger agency," she said. "One that won't screw up your next movie deal."

Peter laughed in spite of what he was feeling.

"I just . . . this new book means a lot to me," he said. "I want to get it right. I need to."

"You will," she said, and, as if tired of talking agents and books, Julianna hooked a hand around the back of his head and pressed her body hard into his. They kissed and lingered together, and his hand found its way to her hip. Peter wanted it never to end, the need to get lost in the taste of her breath, fresh like lemons, her body warm, as he always remembered it. Peter wanted to take her, to press her against the wall and die inside her.

"You know what I'm thinking right now?" Julianna asked, her voice broken by hushed and intimate gasps.

"What?" he said, kissing her neck.

"What I'm in the mood for?"

"I know what I'm in the mood for."

"I can feel what you're in the mood for," she said.

He kissed her again. She looked into his eyes; nothing could ever mean as much.

"Tell me," he said.

"It's different," she said.

"I'm always up for a challenge."

"Okay," she said, her voice a husky whisper. "Lo mein."

"Huh?"

She pushed him back, a twisted smirk on her face. "Y'know, instead of fried rice."

It took him only a beat, but, grinning wildly, Peter lunged after her, wrapping his arms around her waist, tickling her sides, making her scream in delight.

Every Word for Her

His turn to watch from the doorway.

Julianna was in bed, resting against two precariously propped pillows, the white cotton sheet pulled to her waist. She wore a tank top, cotton, ribbed, also white. She bought them in the little-boys' clothing department. Size medium, shrunk in the dryer so as to cling, to emphasize, to rise above her belly button. He could picture the white panties. More cotton. Not a thong, but sort of a string bikini. Nothing sexier for her to wear, at least in Peter's mind. Julianna knew that; he'd told her enough times. It was why she wore them to bed most nights. Though she'd claim comfort, he was pretty damn sure it was because of the effect it had on him—that after so many years of marriage he still could not keep his hands off her.

"I thought she'd never get to sleep," Peter said.

She looked up from her book, making eye contact. A small smile, as if she knew he had been watching, admiring.

"A few days can seem like an eternity when you're that age," she replied.

He made his way to his side of the bed, pulling off his shirt, sitting sideways, so that he wouldn't have to stop looking at her.

"What about you?" he asked. "Did it seem like an eternity?"

"Longer," she replied. "I never want you to go anywhere without me."

"I won't," he said. "I promise I'll never make that mistake again."

"I believe you," she said, closing the book, dropping it onto the nightstand, moving forward, to her knees, grabbing his face, kissing him passionately. Always the aggressor. From their first date, she so beautiful and stoned. He afraid to make that first move.

Pushing him back onto the bed, she climbed on top, her hands pressing at his shoulders as she bit his neck, his nipples, licking her way down his chest.

But the moment Peter clenched his eyes shut they started again.

Flickering, but different this time.

No rolling hubcaps.

But Dina, kneeling before him, taking him into her mouth, eating him alive. Now a cheap stag film for sure. He was watching the images like a horny preteen boy seeing his first naked titties.

Gasping violently, Peter snapped his eyes open. He wouldn't close them again until this was over. He needed to see his wife, to be with his wife. He needed Julianna. To keep her there and not imagine anyone else.

Grabbing her as if he were suddenly a character out of his own imagination, he flipped her onto her back, taking her, making her feel as if she were the only woman who mattered.

Dina

How long had she been there?

How long had she waited?

Standing in the doorway to the basement guitar shop. Huddling in the shadows. Her legs a little numb from not moving, a sharp tingling in her toes as if they wanted to fall asleep. Staring up at the window that she had thought must be his. Knew now for certain *was* his.

Seeing Peter as he walked past, removing his shirt. Not just taking it off, but stripping.

With a purpose.

And Dina knew better than anyone what Peter's purpose was.

She wiped away a tear. Angry. At herself for crying, sure, but . . . she deserved to be up there, in his room, in his bed.

She had had so many visions of what their first time together would be like. And this deception hurt, especially after what happened in Madison. That was supposed to be a preview, a tease, a hint for Peter of what was to come.

Their connection.

Their bond.

She so wanted to be up there now, watching from inside the room. To hear the lies he told her. To smell their sweat.

To scream at her, *Don't you know who he really wants? Don't you know anything at all?*

But understanding that that wasn't a possibility, that she couldn't confront the wife, that wasn't her purpose, not now, not yet, Dina sniffled once, stepped stiffly from the shadows, and, walking east on East Tenth Street, she headed home.

The Mourning Ritual

He leaned against the counter in their small kitchen, against the wood cabinets that barely had enough space for their dishes and some select cereal boxes. The country green of the wood was a nice contrast to the T-shirt he wore over old khakis. The shirt at one point bore the logo of his favorite Los Angeles bookstore on the back, just as at one point it was a hunter green. Now the logo was barely a memory, and the color had faded to a medium gray of sorts, as if all the green had run away. The slacks were old, a little frayed, but okay for home. He was barefoot, the black-and-white linoleum floor cool against the soles of his feet. He held in his hand a mug from a restaurant he could honestly not remember. From it he sipped black coffee.

Peter loved this ritual. Sending the girls off to work was how he thought of it. Kimberly was dressed for school in a blue plaid skirt with white blouse. She was still wearing her cheesehead, its taxicab yellow a stark contrast to her clothes, her surroundings. To life or nature in general. She was being ushered toward the door by her mom, now dressed in her district attorney's suit, navy blue, the skirt falling past her knees, the blouse pale and buttoned all the way, the jacket giving off the opposite effect of one of those white cotton tanks she wore to bed. Her shoes were sensible, stylish but comfortable. Her briefcase soft Coach leather, expensive, a congratulatory present from Peter upon her last promotion.

"Go ahead, ask him," Julianna told her daughter as they approached the kitchen.

"Ask me what, pumpkin?" he asked.

"Can I bring you to show-and-tell?" Kimberly said.

"What?" Peter asked, laughing.

The words came excitedly, a hundred miles per hour. "Sister Bernadette asked us to bring in something to show-and-tell that has to do with what we want to be when we grow up. And Billy Thibeault asked if it was okay to bring in his dad, who's a hockey player for the Rangers, because Billy wants to be a hockey player when he grows up. And she said okay. And then, like, Marissa asked if she could bring in her dad, who's a doctor, 'cause that's what she wants to be." She took a short breath. "And, well, I just thought . . ."

"She's been dying to asking you this for days," Julianna said. "Wouldn't dare do it over the phone."

Peter dropped down to one knee so that he and Kimberly were eye-to-eye. "I would be honored to be your show-and-tell dad," he said, adjusting the yellow foam slab just a little to the right so it sat straight on her head.

"Really?" she said, beaming. "You're not too busy?"

"Never too busy for you."

"Cool!" she said, making it the greatest of all exclamations to her father's ear. "I'll tell Sister Bernadette."

"Okay," he said. "Just let me know when."

"I will."

He stood and smiled at his wife. "How 'bout if I come down to the office . . ."

"So I can show-and-tell you?" Julianna said.

"I was thinking more like taking you to lunch."

"Can't, baby," she said, taking the mug from his hand and grabbing a quick sip of java. "In court all day."

Peter frowned. She handed back the mug and tweaked his cheek.

"See," she said, "it sucks having a real job."

He smiled as they held each other's look.

"Bye, Daddy," Kimberly said, feeling suddenly ignored.

"Bye, Cheesehead," he said.

He kissed them both good-bye, and with Groucho seated by his side, Peter watched them from the doorway of their apartment as they walked to the elevator.

"C'mon, Groucho," he said, shutting the door. "Time to write."

The dog barked once in agreement. But before Peter could even make it out of the kitchen, there was a knock at the door.

"What'd you forget?" he asked, not thinking twice about opening it.

Julianna stepped back through the doorway, grabbing her husband, kissing him so hard on the mouth that he was knocked back two decades. He felt as if he were a teenager again.

"To tell you that last night was great," she said, her voice lusty and blue.

Peter held her close, just listening to their breathing, elongated and tempered, in sync. If one stopped, so would the other.

The voice broke through the rhythm. Annoyed, impatient. "Mommy, can you guys, like, cool it? Please," Kimberly said. "I'm gonna be late."

Smiling, Julianna pulled away from her husband, ever so reluctantly. He gave her a playful slap on the behind, watching as she returned to the elevator, where Kimberly stood against the open door, her arms folded in disgust. Watching as the elevator door slid shut on his waving wife and daughter. Watching until they were gone.

Closing the door, he turned toward the counter, a deep breath caught in his throat, pressing hard against his heart. How could he have cheated on her? Picking up the old Farberware percolator, forever stained by coffee and fingerprints, Peter refilled his mug to the brim with steaming java, knowing there was no easy answer, other than that he'd made a terrible mistake.

He didn't even hear the first clang. Metal against metal, a little hollow, far away, if even real. But the second clang caught his attention. Then another, and one more after that. An unsympathetic beat.

He opened the door, cautiously this time, stepping into the hall in his bare feet. Nothing immediately apparent; the space was too short, too stark. He glanced up and down the flight of stairs opposite the elevator, choosing to follow the sound, to step up.

The metal fire door leading to the roof was slightly ajar, moving with the breeze, clanging against its doorjamb never hard enough to close, just hard enough to bounce back and try again. Hardly a mystery.

Stepping through the door, onto the roof, into the warm September morning sun, Peter looked around, remembering what the view had once been to the south-southwest. The towers always shimmering in light like this. Two pillars of strength and hope. Nothing now to take their place in the sky.

To take their place in his memory.

New Beginning

Peter topped off his coffee, thinking about the rewrite. There were just a few chapters that really needed his attention, some sort of kick, a jump start, some unexpected violence to keep the readers on their toes, turning pages until the very end. Maybe he should call Jeffrey Halliwell and see if he had any connections to murderers. He could picture Halliwell's smirk, answering with a question of his own: "Sure. What kind of murderer do you need?"

Shaking off the thought, unplugging the percolator, which was now drained of his favorite legal drug, Peter picked up his mug and turned. The voice came suddenly, his path blocked.

"Hi."

He was unable to stop quickly; the coffee, steaming, scalding, splashed forward.

"Christ!"

The scream, the blur of motion and color as she clutched at her blouse, pulling it over her head quickly, rushing to the kitchen sink, splashing cold water onto her chest.

His breath heaving, freaked and freakish, turning with her, stepping back, as he yelled, "What the fuck are you doing in my apartment?"

Dina turned to face him then, her blouse tightly balled in one hand, her bra wet and now transparent. Her skin over her left breast was flushed red from the heat of the coffee. Beads of water glistening, rolling down over her stomach.

"Your door was open."

"So, you just walked in?"

"I knocked."

Peter glared at her, letting the rush subside, his breathing calm down. But his mind was racing now, thinking how good she looked, the woman so in his thoughts, the woman he was writing about now, or at least it seemed that way—he needed to shut those thoughts down. Remembering how she felt or, more to the point, how she made him feel—at the moment, then later, how it all made him feel.

Sick.

"How did you even know where I lived?" he asked.

"You told me, remember?" she said. "East Tenth between First and A. Your name's on the buzzer." She reached up to touch his face. "I wanted to see you again, Peter."

He turned in exasperation, pulling back, looking away. "Look, Dina," he said. "What happened in Madison was . . ."

"Just the beginning," she said.

Not Just Anyone

Dina zipped past him suddenly, through the living room, as if rushing from a fire. Or perhaps as if she herself were on fire. Something in her eyes seemed desperate that way.

Peter caught his breath before following after her. Wondering how to get her out of their apartment. How to make sure she never returned. How to make sure Julianna never found out. But no immediate solutions came to mind.

He found her in his office staring at the stained-glass window. Her eyes locked on Mary's, as if these two were sharing a secret. But what could Dina ever have in common with the Virgin Mary? Or perhaps the more disturbing question: What could Mary ever have in common with Dina?

"Just like in the book," she said.

"You have to leave, Dina," he said. "Please."

"I will," she said. "I know I shouldn't be here. But just . . . talk to me for a couple of minutes. Please. Tell me why you made this Angel's bedroom."

He wanted to scream at her to just get out—of his

apartment, his life, his head—but instead Peter found himself explaining.

"I spent so much time in here," he said, "it was just easier to describe reality than make something up." Finding a hangnail on the left side of the middle finger of his right hand, he rubbed at it with the flat of his thumb. "I sent Sam a photo of the window so they could get it right for the play."

Dina took in the room, as if burning every detail into her memory for future use. Watching her, Peter brought the fingernail to his mouth, clamping down with his teeth on the errant piece, ripping it free, opening up a viaduct of crimson. Then, glancing at the gnawed ends of every other nail, never noticing before, he wondered when he had started this habit.

Bending at the knee, Dina pressed on the corner of the left wall's center bookcase, not at all surprised as it popped free, hinging on a spring. She pulled back on the case, opening it like Pandora's box, revealing the hidden storage space. She glanced into the space as if it were magical, reaching in. From it she pulled an old notebook from atop a box once used to house sheets of white bond paper in bulk, now holding all the research and drafts from *Angel*.

Treating the notebook as if it were a Gutenberg Bible, turning back its cover gently, she glanced at the hand-written pages, asking, "What secrets do you have hidden in here?"

Peter answered with a tight smile, then bent forward, taking the book from her hands, taking it away from her as if she had no right. He placed it gently on his desk. "My notes for the first book," he explained.

"Things I'm not allowed to see?" she asked.

"Mostly bad ideas," he said.

Dina straightened up and turned, running a hand over the desktop, picking up the stiletto. She caught her reflection on the blade, pursing her lips, checking her lipstick. Putting it back down, she came to a stop at the new manuscript, and the handcuff paperweight that held it hostage to the corner of Peter's desk.

"The sequel?" she asked.

"One more draft, and it'll be ready," he replied.

Dina lifted the handcuffs and flipped to the first page. "'It was the way they felt against her, like a lover's caress every time she moved,'" she read aloud from chapter one, page one. "'Like lips brushing softly—she could almost feel the wetness of a kiss. Or was that her excitement showing? Angel smiled as she thought that sometimes silk panties made the best lovers.'

"Only sometimes," Dina said, as she turned to smile at Peter.

He let a small puff of air escape his lungs, then glanced at the watch on his left wrist. He was tired of playing her game.

"I probably should get back to work," he said.

Dina flipped the pages back, but didn't return the handcuffs. She pressed her thumb hard against the polished chrome, against the jagged edges of the cuffs' teeth. "Would you let me read it?" she asked, her voice a little hesitant.

"I haven't let anyone read it," Peter replied without hesitation.

"I'm not just anyone," she said.

Peter held her look for a beat, not sure what to say. Did that one drunken night in Madison make her someone special in his life? Someone who'd inevitably change his life?

Dina looked down at the desktop, a small smile playing on her lips. Peter would later recall that she wore the same smile just before dropping to her knees in his room in Madison.

If nothing else, she was consistent.

Slapping the handcuffs suddenly around her wrists, Dina stepped back without warning, closing his office door, slamming back against it now, rising to her toes, stretching her arms high over her head, hooking the cuffs onto an old brass coat hook hung high near the top of the door.

"What are you . . . ?"

"We can pick up where we left off while it's printing out," she said, her words as stretched out as she, a little out of breath, perhaps in anticipation, or discomfort, hanging against the door.

Peter gazed at her, trying to purge the thoughts from his mind. She knew Angel too well, her proclivity toward bondage. Angel liked being tied up because she knew the effect it had on men. It gave them the illusion of control, all smoke and mirrors. And through Angel, Peter lived out desires he'd never have the guts to approach with his wife.

Guts—the difference between them.

Shaking his head, stepping forward, Peter lifted a finger, as if to emphasize a point, as if to say some things were better left to the imagination. But he thought better of it. Dina wouldn't understand. Dina would question why. Instead, he found himself standing too close, fingering the edges of her bra, scalloped lace, rising just over her nipples.

Dina seemed to melt at his touch.

"Is there anything I can't do to you?" he asked, a line from his novel.

A small gasp of air escaped her lips as she stared into his eyes and gave him the sexiest of smirks. "Nothing I can think of at the moment," she replied, just as he expected.

The middle finger of his left hand scooped beyond the lace, running along her goose-bumped flesh on the inside of her bra. Her nipple was hard, and she was trembling.

He thought of so many things to say to her, so many things he wanted to do to her. But instead he tasted bile at the back of his throat, the sour, rancid reminder, and said, "I can't, Dina." He turned away quickly, still catching the burn of disappointment, the devastation in Dina's face, as she stretched some to free the cuffs from the hook.

Lowering her arms, she opened the door. "I'm gonna see if I can get that coffee stain out," she said, hurrying away—from Peter, from his office, from this embarrassment—"so I have something to wear home."

PART TWO

Angel

She scrubbed.

Her fingers raw and bleeding, her arms ragged to the texture of cork, aching, the veins popping—veins popping, did any veins remain? On her knees, always on her knees lately, leaning into the bathtub, pressing into the corroded chrome of the drain. The bristles of her toothbrush pressing into the grime, the scum, the hair, and dried-out, caked-up blood from when he hit her the last time, cut her in places where no one would ever see, but where she would feel, she would wince, because everyone needed to be there. Inside her, the whole world had been inside her.

She hadn't even waited this time. It was her punishment when she'd done wrong. And this time . . . perhaps if he knew she was already sorry, that she had already repented. Prayed for forgiveness by cleaning.

"Dirty stupid junkie whore," she could hear him screaming, the words so burned into her memory that she began to believe them, to accept the pain that went with them.

But it was all she wanted anymore. Gone were all the other pleasures, the other pursuits. Gone were the smiles, the control, her family, her money—nothing left, she had nothing.

Except for the desire to fill her veins.

She couldn't even remember when the sex was fun. The strange natural high that came with tens of thousands of dollars rolled into tight wads filling the belly of a teddy bear.

Gone now.

That high forever faded.

Replaced by the static white noise of the brush against the crud, the corrosive smell of the powered cleanser.

And the dumbfounding fear that echoed the sentiment of How did I get here?

Before He Knew Any Better

Dina scrubbed.

Leaning over the sink, feverishly rubbing the fabric together to the point of fraying. Her favorite blouse ruined. Not by the coffee stain—the coffee stain was long gone—but by the friction, the pressure, her hands, still shackled at the wrists, white-knuckled and raw, the physical pain taking her mind off his rejection.

She knew how to clean.

Peter's words had taught her well.

Guilt stricken so many times over, Peter came up behind her. "How many times have you read *Angel*?" he asked.

A small laugh escaped her throat, then the words, "Why would you care?" before she could stop them, sniffling back a tear that she didn't even realize was there. And when he didn't answer her question, she gave in just as quickly. "Forty-seven times." The number set free a few more tears.

He'd thought about it walking from his office to find her. Who better than Dina to offer an opinion on what he might be doing right or wrong with the new book?

Right or wrong with Angel. It would buy him time, make any contact at least something he could explain. Halfheartedly. She'd become a trusted reader instead of an untrustworthy lover. It wasn't the most bulletproof plan, but at least it would get her out of his apartment.

"You really want to read it?" he asked, wondering if these were words he'd live to regret.

Her hands stopped abruptly, as did the tears. As did the ripping of the arteries pumping pain into her heart. She smiled unconsciously, her back still to Peter.

"I mean now, before it's finished?" he said. "Maybe you could tell me if you think it's on track. The right track."

Dina inhaled deeply, filling her lungs with air. The smile vanished as she turned. She wanted him to understand how seriously she needed this.

"It would mean the world to me," she said, her voice taking on a sincerity that surprised them both.

Peter nodded.

"Okay, then."

"Really?"

Another nod.

"Can I ask for one other thing?"

"What's that?" he said.

Dina held out her handcuffed wrists.

"The key," she said.

With the old laser printer whirring in the background, Peter freed Dina from the handcuffs, his hands shaking— he hoped she hadn't noticed—as he held her wrists, her hands tiny and soft, slipped in the key, and turned.

"I think we're all a little safer with you in handcuffs," he joked.

"You'd be surprised at the damage I could still do," she replied, no appearance of a joke.

Placing the cuffs down on his desk alongside the keys, Peter turned away from her. Bending at the knee, he pressed on the corner of the center bookcase, and opened the storage space. From deep within he pulled out a postal-worn cardboard box. Opening it, its flaps overlapped and tucked into one another, he lifted two folded white T-shirts, silk-screened with the original cover of *Angel*.

"I had a couple dozen of these made up when the book first came out," he said, snapping open one of the shirts, its wrinkles fleeing with the dust of age. "Gave them to friends, mostly, thinking it would help sales." Peter stood. "I was new at this," he said, turning, handing her the shirt. "I have a few left, and I can't think of anyone more deserving of one than the book's biggest fan."

Dina stared in disbelief, looking down then at the shirt as if it were an award of Nobel proportions, a seeming mirror image staring back.

"I don't know what to say."

"Something dry to"—he began, cut short by the vision of her pulling off her bra, snatching the T-shirt out of his hands, and pulling it on over her head—"wear home."

"How's it look?" she asked, smiling.

With her skin still a little wet, the shirt clung to her chest, the white lightweight cotton dissolving to a fleshy pink, dotted with goose bumps.

Peter couldn't take his eyes off her.

"That would have definitely helped sales," he said, immediately wishing he hadn't.

Dina stepped closer. "Maybe you need me around to help you sell the new one," she said, her voice full of promise and longing.

But before Peter could respond, the whir of the printer stopped. The silence caught him by surprise, amplifying the battle raging in his mind. Pushing the volume of his desire to eleven. He knew for certain now that he wanted to fuck her as badly as he wished they'd never met.

Perhaps these feelings were one and the same, a vise squeezing reason like pulp from his heart. The desire to forget. The desire for more. The bridge of guilt between them built with crumbling stone.

"Maybe you should read it first," he said.

Running Away in Reverse

Closing the apartment door, Peter listened for the elevator taking Dina down, taking her away. He locked the dead bolt, leaning forward, banging then pressing his forehead hard against the doorjamb. The painted wood, a little worn, a lot chipped, felt cold and brittle against his skin. Like rough nails scratching. He wished for it to hurt more.

Returning to his office, he took a seat behind his desk and stared at the computer screen, at the title page of his new book: *It's a Wonderful Lie*, a novel by Peter Robertson.

Maybe Dina can help, he thought. Unlock some clue, some mystery to Angel that he had yet to discover. Or give him a push in the right direction. A hint at those violent urges that he could not completely comprehend. Or maybe the manuscript would simply bore her, end her obsession, allow her to let go of his character and be done with them both.

"Who the fuck am I kidding?" he whispered, looking up at the stained-glass window. The Virgin Mary gazed down in disapproval, as if she believed the only reason

Peter gave Dina the manuscript was to keep her around that much longer.

He was tall, wearing a hoodie pulled tight against his features, dark glasses to cover his eyes. Bloodied and startled, he held on to a corner light post, his fingers gripping it. Shaking his head, snapping it back, his body falling, he began to walk backward, on shaky legs, tentative but urgent.

As if running away in reverse.

Mike Levine

It was a shiny and new skyscraper on Madison Avenue in the mid-fifties. Mirrored glass puncturing the sky. A peek of St. Patrick's towers from the right angle, and Atlas with the world on his shoulders if you squinted. A fancy leather boutique on the first floor, next door to the world's largest candy store.

Peter rode the elevator to eighteen. His agent's office was to the left, opposite a small publishing house that specialized in cookbooks.

He pushed through the double glass doors, the words THE LEVINE LITERARY AGENCY in a masculine gold-leaf font, into a small waiting room with hard leather sofas and copies of *Publishers Weekly* and *Kirkus* dotting the Norwegian end tables.

A blonde, in her mid-twenties, tall, stacked, showing just enough cleavage, looked up as Peter entered. It took a beat before she recognized him and stood, a beaming smile crossing her face.

"Peter?" she said, a shriek of delight in her voice. "Oh, my God!"

"Sandra," he replied, trying to match her excitement.

"It's been much too long," she said, reaching out to take his hand as he approached her desk, then squeezing it warmly.

"Yes, it has," Peter replied.

"How are you?"

"I'm good," he said, wondering if she'd really like to know what was going on in his mind right now. "And you?"

"Oh, you know," she replied, rolling her eyes toward her boss's office. "Nothing ever changes around here."

"Is that a good thing?"

"Depends," she said, her tone seeming to take on some other, much heavier meaning. "I'm not sure any of us deal very well with change."

Peter nodded. He wouldn't argue that point.

"He in?"

"For you? Absolutely," she said, lifting the receiver on her phone, about to punch a button.

"Let me surprise him," Peter said, stopping her.

Her tone got serious. "Mike doesn't like surprises."

"Do you?" Peter asked, surprising himself with the question.

A small laugh escaped her throat. She was as shocked as he was, looking at him differently, then speaking with a tone in her voice he had never heard before. "What do you think?"

Peter held her look for a beat. He remembered the first time he saw Sandra, about four years back now. She was fresh out of college. A Smith graduate. BA in twentieth-century literature. *A smart young thing*, was how Mike once referred to her. Sandra was always smiling, always making you feel attractive, as if you had a chance. She left a lasting impression on any straight male writer who walked through that door. Peter was pretty sure that was why she had the job.

"Go ahead." She gave in. "Get me fired."

"Like that's going to happen," he said, pretty damn sure this smart young thing would be slapping a sexual harassment suit on Mike Levine's ass if she ever left not of her own volition.

Perhaps that was why Peter liked her.

"Got a minute?"

He was leaning back in his Aeron chair, barking into his Bluetooth headset, his back to the door, spinning around at the intrusion. Mike Levine, all Armani and greed, was about to bite the intruder's head off, then give Sandra a well-worn "What the hell are you doing?" until he recognized Peter.

"I'll call you back," he said, cutting off the call without warning, pulling off the headset, standing, grinning wildly, his arms open wide and friendly.

"Am I seeing a fucking ghost?" Mike said. "Or is that really you?"

Peter stepped forward, shaking his agent's hand. He wasn't really sure what to say. The words felt a little jumbled. It had been almost a year since they last spoke. Maybe longer. Peter's doing. He wasn't ready; the book wasn't ready. And what else was there to talk about?

"You look good," Mike said.

"I, um . . . yeah. I feel good," Peter said, thinking now that this was a bad idea. He had no time for small talk, for playing catch-up. He had a book to finish. "I figured I owed you a visit."

Nodding, and with a small laugh, Mike sat back

down, crossing his legs, giving a tug on the crease of his pants leg to smooth out any wrinkles. Peter was reminded how it was all about appearances. The photo on his own book jacket—a snapshot taken by Julianna not good enough. A photo shoot had been arranged. A pretentious British photographer who had over a hundred *Vogue* pictorials under his belt and was a frequent guest on some modeling reality television show. Mike standing in the background showing the first-time author how to pose. Peter hated the photograph. "That's not me," he remembered telling his wife when the proofs arrived.

"Maybe not," she had replied, trying to make him feel better, "but he's damn cute."

Mike motioned toward the two matching Aerons in front of his desk. Peter sat in the one closest to the door.

"So," Mike said.

"Yeah, so."

"You're ready to move on?"

"Without question," Peter replied. "This has been"—he searched for the right word, and only one came immediately to mind—"difficult."

"Difficult is my specialty," Mike said. "Or do I have to remind you how no publishers at first were interested in *Angel*?"

"You have," Peter said. "Plenty of times. You just did again."

"It bears repeating," Mike said. "No problems I can't take care of."

"A regular miracle worker."

"Abso-fucking-lutely," Mike said, laughing, cutting to the chase. "When do I get to see it?"

"I'm in the middle of the final draft now," Peter said. "Give me another week or so."

"That fast?" Mike asked.

"It's all coming together," Peter replied.

Mike followed Peter out of his office, giving him a hearty pat on the shoulders. A friendly enough gesture.

"It's been forever since we've hung out," Mike said.

"Yes, it has," Peter said. Not that he'd missed it. *Hanging out* meant one thing to Mike, and that so wasn't Peter's scene.

"So, let's grab pizza, get shit-faced . . ."

". . . end up at Scores?"

"You're reading my mind," Mike said.

He nodded, catching the roll of Sandra's eyes as he gave Mike a tight but friendly smile.

"It's one-track," Peter said.

Cheesehead

A sea of blue plaid against monastery stone as the bell fractured the wail of a siren screeching to destinations unknown, the sound bouncing down West Eleventh Street like the institutionalized off the wall.

The children who attended St. Ovilia's, first through fifth graders, rushed past with cries of freedom, their own personal redemption songs. Kimberly was among them, still wearing the cheesehead. She found her dad waiting for her by the old wrought-iron gate. He was looking down, away from the unfriendly stares of mothers and nannies who must have never forgiven him for writing *Angel*, such filth in their eyes, as if every fifteen-year-old junkie escort were his invention.

Peter avoided their scorn by peeling chips off the layers of Rust-Oleum, black and bubbly in spots, the rust hiding underneath nonetheless. He wondered how many times this particular gate had been painted. And did the layers of black do more to protect the iron or the rust, like blinders, black-colored glasses—what we can't see can never affect us?

He looked up as Kimberly approached, running into

his arms. "Don't tell me you had that on all day," he said, lifting her toward the sky.

"Okay," she said, giggling, "I won't tell you."

Laughing, Peter kissed his daughter's forehead, his own bumping against the yellow foam from Wisconsin. Then he placed her gently back down, taking her hand.

"Did you have a good day at school?" he asked.

"Yesh," she replied, the air whooshing through a missing front tooth. "We had a spelling test, and I got all the words right."

"Cool," he said.

"C-O-O-L," she spelled. "And y'know what?"

"What?"

"Sister Bernadette said I could bring you to show-and-tell."

"Oh, yeah, when?" Peter asked.

"Two weeks from tomorrow," she said.

"I'll make sure I send my writing suit to the dry cleaner's so it's all nice and clean."

Kimberly laughed. "You're silly, Daddy."

"I know," he said.

The mothers and nannies weren't looking anymore; they weren't watching. Most had simply picked up their kids and gone home, shaking their heads as they passed. In denial.

Peter and Kimberly were the last to walk away from the school. They usually were, taking their time. Especially on beautiful early fall days such as this, echoes of summer still lingering.

The few trees yet to turn.

She watched from across the street. Smoking. Enjoying every wretched drag. How miserable she'd become since New York went smoke-free. An end to her Scotch and sodas and a couple of Camel nonfilters, and maybe some buffalo wings, in her favorite bar after a particularly grueling shift. She tried it at home, but it wasn't the same. It felt desperate, lonely. And in her mid-forties, twice divorced, Paula Rossi didn't need any help in that direction.

She stayed, leaning back against the side of her car, until Peter Robertson turned a corner and disappeared from view. After sucking on the Camel until there was nothing left to hold, and she'd need a roach clip to pull another drag, she tossed the stub to the ground, twisting it dead with the toe of her shoe.

Adjusting her jacket as she got into her car, an unmarked Ford, just in time to hear the radio squawk a two-eleven, armed robbery, three blocks north.

"On my way," NYPD Detective First-class Rossi said out loud to no one in particular. There was no one else in the car. No one was listening.

She did that a lot lately, she thought, talk to herself. Shaking her head, wondering if it was a sign that she was finally losing it—her last husband insisted she'd lost it—she slapped a rotating light onto the roof of her car, its magnetic base holding it in place. Then Detective Rossi took off in the direction of the crime, speaking to no one now.

Not even herself.

Disney World

He wasn't much of a cook. Back in the bachelor days, those college years, cooking meant no money for even the rankest fast food, but ramen noodles, on sale, five packages for a dollar, boiled, seasoned with salt, or pepper, or whatever was available. He remembered dousing the noodles with ketchup from little packets he'd taken from the hot-dog stand just off campus, hoping for something resembling pasta with red sauce, but not even coming close.

If he had a few dollars in his wallet, he'd opt to eat out. A slice of pizza, the cheapest burger on McDonald's menu—anything was better than hitting the stove. Peter just didn't have the flair for cooking. He barely had the flair for boiling water—twice he'd left a teakettle alone, burner on medium, retreating to his office to write, to forget about the boiling water, only to return a few hours later to find the stainless-steel pot glowing red. He gave up tea altogether.

"Won't Mommy be surprised?" he asked his daughter as he slipped on an oven mitt and pulled a large wooden spoon from a drawer of utensils.

In lieu of a reply, Kimberly asked, "You feeling okay, Daddy?"

Peter laughed. "I'm fine, pumpkin. Never been better."

The timer chirped, a persistent electronic ping that cut through any wall of sound. Peter unsuccessfully pushed at the button to shut it off. He tried again, but despite the button's label—STOP—it continued to chirp.

"You're pushing the wrong button, Daddy," Kimberly said; then, reaching around him, she pressed the button marked START and said, "There."

The chirping stopped.

Shrugging it off, needing no explanation other than that this was a world in which he did not belong, Peter swung open the door to the oven.

Kimberly peered into the smoky confines. "What is it?" she asked.

"Baked ziti," he said. "Doesn't it look good?"

"You really want me to answer that?" she replied, making a face, because even at six, Kimberly was pretty certain pasta wasn't supposed to look like that.

Julianna smiled as she raised a forkful to her mouth, nibbling at the corner of a penne tube, biting off the cheese, or what she assumed to be cheese.

Peter grimaced at his first bite.

Kimberly just pushed her plate away.

"Really, honey," Julianna said, "it's the thought that counts."

It was the way they'd lived their lives: emphasis on the little things. The surprises from the heart, tellingly intimate. The bag of chocolate Kisses after a losing battle in court. A kooky PEZ dispenser to make him laugh. Letting her pick the movie, or letting him pick the movie, or skipping the movie altogether for a walk in Central Park as the first winter snow began to fall. Sharing their time, planning their time, so that togetherness was always at the top of their to-do lists.

"We could get pizza," Peter conceded.

"Yea! Pizza!" Kimberly screamed.

"There's nothing wrong with this," Julianna said, smiling at her husband, taking another bite. "I like my pasta . . . *blackened*."

He leaned against the doorjamb that had once held a swinging door separating the kitchen from the living room, removed and most likely discarded by the previous owner for reasons Peter could only surmise. He watched her as he sipped from a glass of wine that helped mask the taste of the dinner that they had all somehow managed to plow through.

Julianna sat on the sofa, the middle pillow of three. It was where she always sat, so that she could be surrounded on both sides by those who meant the most to her. Staring at the TV, holding her left wrist with her right hand, unconsciously twisting an old charm bracelet around her wrist. Sterling silver and a little tarnished, it was a cherished gift from her maternal grandmother. Something she wore every day. It was one of the first things Peter had noticed about her, when he got past the obvious and started in on the details. The way she'd pull it around her wrist, each charm another step on the never-ending circle.

He sat by her side now. The right pillow. He put his arm around her as she lay her head on his shoulder, like puzzle pieces interlocking.

Julianna pointed at the TV. Peter looked. It was a

home video from a little over a year ago. The three of them on vacation. Against his better judgment, he fell into the parenthood trap, allowing their at-the-time five-year-old daughter to cast the deciding vote on that particular trip. And despite himself, Peter had a blast. Both he and Julianna felt like children again, three five-year-olds armed with a platinum American Express card running amok.

"When you sell this book," she asked, "do we get another trip to Disney World?"

He kissed her forehead, thinking of the little things. Thinking he really wanted to feel five again, especially now.

"Anywhere you want to go," he said.

Repetition

Peter had lost track of time.

It happened a lot when he was writing, pulling a late shift once Julianna had drifted off to sleep and his only options left were to read or stare at the ceiling until he couldn't keep his eyes open anymore. He didn't read much when writing. Not after staring at words all day—or all night—long. Other people's words would swim, would burn. Would make him believe he had it all wrong.

One make-believe world at a time.

Drifting into his office, he did a quick e-mail check, mainly offers of credit cards and prescription drugs, their names just a little askew so as to get past the spam filters. He was about to log off, his mailbox going from fifty-six entries to none, when that familiar computerized voice forewarned him of a fresh entry: He had mail. Though he expected to hit DELETE on what was probably at this time of the night some offer of porn or a pyramid scheme from a third-world nation, the subject line caught his attention.

Thinking of you, it read.

The sender's e-mail address: MadisonDina.

Peter still so wanted to ignore the message, to hit DELETE and forever condemn it to some cyberspace recycle bin. Let some lonely computer geek discover it, discover her, absolve Peter of his misery. But instead he clicked READ.

His first guess was right: It was pornographic. He was the star of Dina's little fantasy, written in Angelspeak, using his character's slang, her rhythm. It was almost as if Peter wrote it himself, into a first draft, only to delete it later after a trusted reader commented that it was too over-the-top. Graphic in its detail, scratching at the depths of his desire, scratching at what he might never have even fantasized. What she would do to him, for him, if only given the opportunity.

Again unable to hit DELETE, he closed down the e-mail, saving it to a folder where he stored research for *Angel*. He knew he'd want to read it again, or perhaps use it, incorporate it into the new book, or the one after that. So it could be cut in later rewrites when the trusted reader would once again tell him, *Leave it to the reader's imagination.*

Opening his word-processing program, Peter pulled up the latest version of *It's a Wonderful Lie*. The file name: lie-v02.wpd. Version two, his self-imposed rewrite. He did a go-to jump to page 178, chapter thirty-six—keep them short. It was a section of the book that had been bothering him. It wasn't playing right; Angel wasn't playing right. The motivation for her revenge. Peter wondered if he were making it clear.

He stared at the computer screen, the words in twelve-point Courier font. Lifting his fingers from the keyboard, Peter picked up the pair of handcuffs from the desktop, closing one of the bracelets against a non-existent wrist, the steel teeth clicking, pressing through, tighter, smaller than the wrists of a newborn, until nothing, freedom, the hook of the bracelet swinging free, then around and back again, the first steel tooth catching, captured again. He repeated the action, over and again, slapping the cuff lightly against his thigh, the few links of chain sounding like a desperate tambourine keeping time with the rhythm of the clicks.

Dina

She wore the T-shirt still. Nothing else at the moment, but she was alone, in bed. The T-shirt was comfortable. The T-shirt was comforting. The T-shirt would suffice.

Downing what was left of some Cointreau on ice, mainly ice at this point, softened and sweet, Dina sat back on a few large pillows, tucked her toes under the white cotton sheets, then lifted Peter's new manuscript off her nightstand. Pulling it onto her lap, she touched the title page lightly. Reading, mouthing the words, *It's a Wonderful Lie*, a novel by Peter Robertson, the date of the draft, his address and phone number, the copyright info. *All rights reserved.*

Taking a deep breath, fingering the edge of the page, twenty-pound bond, crisp, white—how could something so delicate slice through flesh? She flipped the page, her features freezing, then hardening for a beat. A sudden gasp of cold running through her veins. She had an answer, at least. It wasn't the paper that could cut, but the words.

"'For Julianna and Kimberly, every word, always, for you,'" she read out loud from the dedication page.

"I don't think so" was her immediate reply, as she crumpled the page into a tight ball, holding it in her fist as if to suffocate, to wring all life from the phrase.

Turning away then from *Chapter One*, the words she had been expecting to see, Dina locked her eyes on the pink Princess phone next to her alarm clock, in front of her lamp. It was vintage and clunky, two dollars at a local thrift shop, and so like the one she remembered from home. It had a loud ring, a real bell. And she liked the old-fashioned rotary dial.

It was slow, deliberate.

It made you think twice while placing a call.

Exciting Offers

It was a concentration like no other. Perhaps threading a needle or brain surgery came closest. Playing God on a PC, creating life, death, heartbreak, happiness. Misery.

Wrestling with the one word that would best get the point across. Punishing it, confusing it, perhaps misusing it or musing it over. Reworking a simile to make it as invincible as it was invisible, seamless, right. Peter was trying to describe what Angel was feeling the moment she discovered the deception, when his phone rang, shattering concentration like a ninety-nine-mile-per-hour fastball through a paned glass window.

"Christ!" he yelled, his heart racing suddenly as if toward extinction. He clutched his chest, short of breath. When was he ever short of breath?

Snatching up the wireless receiver. "Hello!" His tone neither polite nor friendly. Even less so when he was greeted by silence, forced to repeat himself. "Hello. Is anyone there?"

About to hang up when, "Hi," came the voice from the phone, "this is David from Verizon, and I'm calling to tell you about an exciting new offer that will change the way you make long-distance calls."

Peter didn't notice her appearance in the doorway to his office. Leaning up against the jamb as always, watching him from behind. Otherwise he might have softened his approach.

"Do you have any fucking idea what time it is?" he yelled, hanging up, slamming the phone against his desk, wishing it were old-fashioned with a bell so that it would have clanged with the force with which he slammed the receiver into its cradle. Technology did have a way of watering down drama.

"Telemarketer?" Julianna asked, perhaps a little bemused.

Peter spun around quickly, as if to ward off an attack. Catching himself, reeling back the emotions.

"What? Oh, right. Yeah," he muttered, forcing a laugh, or maybe it was just all jangly nerves.

Peter's head throbbed as he turned back to stare at the phone, half expecting it to ring again, as she came over to rub his shoulders.

"I think you scared him away," she said.

He rolled his head into the movement of her hands. There was nothing to compare to her touch.

"Someone's tense," she said.

"Tough scene," Peter said, reaching for the mouse, needing a break from the words, minimizing the file.

"Want to talk about it?"

"Do I ever?"

"No, but . . . I always ask."

She did always ask. Just as Peter never spoke about it, never wanted to. The emotions of his characters, too raw, too familiar. His. Sometimes hers. What he knew best, what he felt, what frightened him most. A crushing loss.

"Angel realizes she needs to kill someone she once trusted," he heard himself explaining.

The massage stopped, just Julianna's hands now, resting on his shoulders, one finger rising to touch lightly at his earlobe, until Peter spun around in his chair to face her.

"It's hard to kill someone you know," he said.

Julianna reached for his hand. "C'mon to bed," she said. "I think you've worked enough for one night. I'll take your mind off the book; you can start fresh in the morning."

Peter pulled her suddenly and roughly so that she landed on his lap.

"Take my mind off it right here," he said.

"In your office?" she asked.

He reached forward then, a quick flash of steel—the handcuffs, slapping them onto his wife's wrists. Her eyes went wide, and her breath caught in her throat, that little gasp of air when he caught her by surprise, which wasn't that often, turning her on in a way she didn't quite comprehend, as if she wasn't even aware of this particular fantasy. Or hadn't ever imagined it. How he could still surprise her, after so many years.

"I don't know what's gotten into you," she said, leaning close, kissing him, biting at his top lip.

"But you like it, don't you?" he said.

"So far," she replied.

Dina

Her hands shook like those of a junkie holding the fix that could set things right.

Still chapter one. Page one.

Still not quite ready.

Dina flipped the title page back into place, thinking twice. She turned away from the manuscript, the deep blue eyes of a now-dead rock star catching hers. Her first crush, her first true love. One self-inflicted rifle shot to the head and any chance of that future came crashing down. But a poster of his face was still worthy of a few square feet of wall space. Especially now, in memory of things that could never have been. A eulogy for puppy love.

Taking a deep breath, turning to her peanut gallery of stuffed friends on the bookcases that lined the wall opposite her bed. The oldest, the wisest, a king-size teddy bear dressed in bib overalls. Mr. Greenjeans, she called him, though the overalls were blue. Nothing, in fact, on the outside, would warrant his name.

Dina sat on her bed, smiling across the room at the teddy, the oval stained-glass window over her head casting a surrealistically serene depiction of the Virgin Mary on the closest white wall. The deeper shades of the stained glass paling to pastels in the moonlight. Her bed was under the window in the way Peter's desk was. So appropriate.

She placed the manuscript aside, putting it down on her desk in the same spot upon which it rested on Peter's, close to the rear left edge, now so close to the notebook, the old *Angel* notebook. While he was digging for that *Angel* T-shirt, she'd covered it with manuscript pages to his unfinished novel, hot off the printer, stealing the decisions that had made his novel come so alive.

Angel was real. She was Angel. This was their birth certificate.

Picking up a psychology magazine she'd purchased from an East Village street vendor for a quarter, along with a pair of scissors, Dina made herself comfortable on her bed. Flipping through the pages, glancing not at photographs or illustrations, but at the words, the headlines, searching for the article that made her splurge in the first place. Found it on page eighty-eight; it was entitled: "The Peter Principle." She used the scissors to cut the word *Peter* from the page.

Dina stared then at the word, at his name, lying flat in the palm of her hand, as if he were something she could attain, own, crush, a future so bright. She then tossed the magazine aside, where it landed atop a hefty pile of other discarded periodicals.

Standing, snatching a small bottle of brush-on glue from her desk, Dina went to the bookcase, dropping to her knees as she stared for a beat into Mr. Greenjeans's brown button eyes, pressing on a lower shelf. A click as it popped back and opened like a gateway. Leaning in, she grabbed a flashlight to illuminate the space, entering, closing the secret door behind her.

Curled tightly, her knees pressed to her chest, she searched for an empty spot. Finding one finally, a tight squeeze, she glued the word to the wall. Seeing how its letters, its font, differed from its neighbors. She had lost count of how many. How many times she'd cut his name. How many times she'd papered it to the walls of this so-personal space. How many times she'd read each one aloud. How many hours she'd spent in this coffin of sorts, surrounded by only him.

Flights Canceled Due to Fog

Unable to sleep, too frightened to dream, Peter found himself back in front of his monitor, hands on the keyboard, middle finger of his right hand holding steadfast to the DELETE button.

The letters disappeared in reverse order of how he'd just typed them: D-E-T-N-A-W space L-E-G-N-A space G-N-I-H-T space T-S-A-L space. That middle finger smacking hard against the key, three last times, E-H-T, a fuck-you to the inspiration that so seemed to be lacking.

He might as well blame the computer.

Shaking his head in disgust at the white screen now. Only the chapter title remained. But chapter titles weren't the problem. If novels could consist of chapter titles, he'd have a dozen or so books under his belt by now. It was the sentences that came next, that filled in the spaces between those titles.

He pushed hard on his desk, rolling back in his chair, almost to the opposite wall, slouched low, bad for his posture.

What was missing?

Whenever he'd been inspired for the first book, he'd

jot the idea, the turn of a phrase, the simile, some back-breaking quote down in a notebook that never left his hands.

Was the inspiration missing? Or the notebook?

There was none for *It's a Wonderful Lie.* It was all in his head. Or at least, that was where it was supposed to be. Where he wished it were. When his head wasn't fogged over. But at times like these, flights were being canceled.

He didn't want to say he was stuck. He didn't believe in writer's block. That was little more than an excuse for laziness, or a cover for the realization that the person blocked wasn't a writer after all.

Thinking some old inspiration might breed the new, Peter rolled over to the storage space, pressing the left top corner with his knee. A click, and the door snapped forward a few inches. Just enough for Peter to pull at the now-exposed latch.

Dropping off the chair to one knee, he reached in for the old notebook. It should have been resting atop the box holding the research and drafts from *Angel.*

He'd just seen it, touched it, moved it.

But the notebook wasn't there.

Immigrant Bride

Lying in bed now, long past the point of wishing for nightmares and creatures hiding under the bed. No longer caring about the notebook, or the novel. Wanting just to put it all out of his mind. Peter turned onto his side, his focus switching from the relatively long distance of the ceiling to the night table so nearby. His eyes ached. He realized reading glasses weren't in his near future. They were in his here and now. Ten-point type needed to be held at arm's length. The fine-print index of the three-inch-thick video guide was unreadable.

Julianna's charm bracelet rested on the closest corner of the distressed-maple night table. He was eyeing now the small silver Christmas tree, adorned with pinprick-size red and green gemstones pressed into its hand-carved branches. The tree had landed perfectly on its base when Julianna had placed the bracelet down. It seemed to sprout now from the night table as if having taken root. Next to the tree, on its side, as if at the conclusion of some horrible accident, was an old British convertible, an MG or Triumph; it was hard to distinguish at this scale.

Peter picked out his one addition to this antique, a hardcover book, opened flat at about its halfway mark, the words *I love you* engraved in script on its pages. He couldn't read the words from his vantage point on the pillow, but he knew they were there—like the bracelet itself on the night table, where Julianna placed it every night just before getting into bed—they always would be.

Peter could picture her actions. Sitting on the edge of the bed, wearing whatever white cotton she chose for that night's tease, her toes pressed against the hardwood floors, feet arched, like her back. She'd stretch and then slip off the bracelet. Anything else Peter would have to remove. She'd place it, not in a clump of silver, but in a perfect circle, as if in the showcase window of the jewelry shop where it first caught her grandfather's attention, and he bought it for his young immigrant bride, filling its bangles when he could with trinkets of his love. Julianna would scoot back, pulling those miraculous legs under the covers, as she patted a pillow down behind her back and pulled a magazine or book from her nightstand, while waiting for Peter to come to bed.

He'd asked her once why she always put it on his night table and not hers.

"So if I wake up in the middle of the night," she had replied, "I can see both of you at the same time."

Just beyond Julianna's charm bracelet was a combo phone/clock radio, which Peter had owned since his college days. The radio had laughable reception, with its bright orange line he'd slide across the frequency band, trying to find some station, any station, so a voice or music could wake him instead of some persistent beep. The light from the clock readout was a blue so bright, Peter could actually read by it in the otherwise dark of night. Julianna had often suggested replacing the contraption with something more modern. But it was like an old favorite shirt to Peter. Or old jeans. Something he couldn't just yet part with.

He always did have trouble letting go.

The Apology

Usually a walk with Groucho first thing in the morning cleared his head. They'd jaunt through Tompkins Square Park, then to wherever else nature might take them. This morning nature seemed to lead Groucho back home.

Turning off Avenue A onto Tenth Street, heading west, he spotted her from three brownstones away. She was sitting on the steps to his building. Third step up from the sidewalk. The far side of the stairs, so tenants could pass. She watched him as he approached, as if she knew from which direction he'd be coming. She smiled, then stood, pressing out with her hands the nonexistent wrinkles in her almost nonexistent skirt.

What was it about Dina? Peter thought, wishing he could hide, or die, or disappear all at once. If he had created her, why couldn't he make her go away?

"Hi," she said.

Peter nodded. "Don't tell me you've finished it already," he managed, hoping the visit was about the new book. Hoping she'd have an idea that might spark a typing frenzy.

"Actually," she said, "I haven't started it yet. I wasn't ready. There was something I needed to do first."

Peter could feel himself tense up. Frightened, as if a gun were pressed to his head, a holdup in desperation at a 7-Eleven off the Garden State Parkway. Three a.m., the clerk already dead. All he'd wanted was a bottle of cold water. And now there'd be no one around for miles to hear him die.

"What's that?" he asked, not wanting to know.

"Apologize," Dina said.

Holding her look, thinking about the power in that act of contrition. The simple words *I'm sorry*. The freedom they bought us. From ourselves mostly. Lifting that burden of guilt.

Before he could respond, the front door to his building opened. A familiar face appeared. Not cheery, or friendly, or even happy to see him. Just familiar, as in Mrs. Waters had been living in Peter's building when he first moved in. She had lived there since before he was born. Probably before his father was born. She was as much a fixture as the plumbing, or the wires pulsing electrical current like blood through veins keeping the building alive. She was the building's first gray-hair.

"Mrs. Waters," he said, masking what outward guilt he might have felt about being seen with Dina in public. "How are you today?"

She answered with a scowl, shooting him a look as if he were a crazy man, as if he were dirty, as if she could read the guilt in his eyes. What right had he to call her name out loud?

Pushing past, walking slowly yet in exaggerated stumps down the stairs, gripping the black wrought-iron railing, squeezing it white, Mrs. Waters hobbled down the street. A limp, favoring her left side. The soles of her white orthopedic shoes squishing like wet sponges against the sidewalk.

He waited until she was out of earshot, an eternity of geriatric baby steps, then said, "What do you have to apologize for?"

Dina waited a beat herself, watching not Peter's elderly neighbor, but Peter. "Coming on too strong," she said.

"It was wrong," he said.

It was what he'd been thinking since slamming that door to his hotel shut. But there was no guilt to be lifted. The guilt was welded to his steel frame, protected by side-impact air bags.

"I know that now. But"—she shrugged, lowered her voice, sounding now like the teenage Angel, conspiring with a friend—"let's just pretend it never happened."

He nodded slowly. "You come on strong, Dina."

"No regrets, remember? You see something you want, take it."

"Just like Angel?"

"The words by which I live," she said.

"A frightening thought, but . . ." Peter nodded a few times, wondering if it could be so simple as to end here. But what choice did he have, really? "Apology accepted."

"Good," she said, beaming. "And please know, if you ever change your mind . . ."

"About?" he asked, refusing even to acknowledge the offer. Offended by her persistence.

She held his inquisitive look for a beat, knowing he knew full well, then, shaking her head, said, "Never mind. I've got a book to read."

"And I've got a rewrite to finish."

Nodding, Dina leaned up and gave him a slightly lingering kiss on the cheek.

A kiss good-bye, he hoped.

And catching his look, she blushed.

"Damn," she whispered, pulling herself back from the arms that weren't holding her, turning, and hurrying aimlessly down the block.

"I'll call you when I'm through," she yelled back over her shoulder. "Let you know if you're on track."

Peter gave her a little wave good-bye, watching her walk away with only one thought playing in his head: She wasn't going away anytime soon.

Something in the Water

Julianna hurried off to work with their daughter in tow. At least she wasn't wearing the cheesehead today, Peter thought as he sipped his coffee.

"Bye, Daddy," Kimberly said.

"See ya later, pumpkin," he replied.

Julianna gave her husband a kiss flush on the mouth, holding the sides of his face with both hands.

"Someone could use a shave," she said.

It had been a few days. Since returning home from Madison. But then, he had been writing. And when he was writing, everything fell to the wayside for Peter. Life was put on hold. If it weren't for Julianna he probably wouldn't even shower, or barely eat. Just coffee and the words, and maybe a strong shot of Jack Daniel's at night to kill the caffeine high.

He smiled. "Make a deal with you," he said. "I'll shave if you shave."

A shocked but sexy grin overtook Julianna's features. She held on to his look as she calculated that it was a win-win situation.

"Deal," she said, kissing him again, then whispering, "What do they put in the Madison water?"

"The Viagra factory is out there," Peter joked. "All the waste gets tossed into the reservoir."

"Let's move," came her reply.

Hot water first.

Softened the whiskers, made the scrape of the blade seem less torturous, less like self-flagellation. Peter never could get the hang of an electric. There was nothing close to the shave of a blade, no matter the commercials that claimed otherwise. A razor was the way to go, if you wanted to feel.

Onto his palm he dropped a dollop of gel, which turned a lighter shade, less translucent before he could even slap it on. A menthol sting, rubbing in circles over his cheeks, chin, the space over his upper lip, down his neck, as if the order would never change.

He held the triple blade of the razor under the streaming water, as hot as the tap could go. Hot enough so that the mirror clouded over in protest. In theory the hot blade would melt off the whiskers, slice through them like a hot knife through butter.

In theory.

The journey began by his right ear, upward against the grain, toward his hairline. Then down, and sideways, a little forward toward the front of his face. It was a country drive over hilly back road. But there was always a surprise around the bend, a deer, a freakish summer storm, an SUV headed right at you.

Rounding his chin next he felt the sting. The blood mixing with the foam, a lighter shade of red, but still bloody enough to make out in the mirror among the shades of gray.

Peter's hands were shaking suddenly. It hurt to breathe. He dropped the razor, the snap-on blade bouncing off upon impact with the porcelain, and held on to the sides of the sink as if the world were crumbling down around him, as if the floor had just given way, and his muscles were tearing from the strain of holding it all together.

That's what remembering was like.

Raoul

The neighborhood had that lingering smell of garbage and vomit. Perhaps that should have been his warning.

Peter was off on his quest. Research, he called it. But he wondered now, at this point, if he'd be doing it anyway, without a first novel to write. As if that first taste of this foreign world, hints of which were so vivid on the Internet, were proving irresistible. The curiosity having its way with him.

With a messenger bag slung over his shoulder, its leather all buff and new, its image so very downtown at that point in time, a claim that he wasn't a nine-to-fiver anymore, Peter located the address Jeffrey Halliwell had pointed him toward. Third Street, just off Avenue D. You couldn't go much farther east. Alphabet City the way it used to be.

He pressed a buzzer for the basement apartment and waited, taking a glance over his shoulder, wondering if this was a place where any life-form should stand still. Watching a homeless man glare at him from under the brim of a baseball cap, his eyes white to the point of no return. A low-slung Toyota, its windows blackened, gliding slowly past, the bass-heavy thud of a song that was too loud to recognize. The teenagers walking by, all attitude and sweat, laughing at him as if he hadn't a clue.

No, Peter thought to himself, as he heard the first of many locks click free, this was a place to keep moving.

Raoul was a large man. Not as tall as Peter, but somehow he managed to tower over him. His arms and thighs bulging and juiced under a baggy athletic shirt and shorts. He looked as if he could pick his teeth with Peter, if he were so inclined.

Raoul took one look at the novelist-to-be, chuckled once to himself, then pulled the door all the way open so Peter could pass.

"Can you be more white?" he asked, slamming the door shut, the locks falling back into place.

Peter didn't answer; he didn't feel as if he were expected to. Instead he took in his surroundings, a veritable den of technology, things that had yet to be invented. A television the size of a billboard took up one wall, its image so crisp he felt he could steal the ball from the NBA players dribbling downcourt. The sound in three-sixty, the slap of that ball on the hardwood, the drip of a player's sweat. Raoul didn't want to watch; he wanted to participate.

"You wearing a wire?"

The voice came from behind him. A question he was expected to answer. Peter turned. His face must have given his fear away.

"A wire?" he answered. "No."

"Arms up," Raoul ordered.

"Excuse me?" Peter said, not sure what he meant. No one had ever said, "Arms up," to him before, except for perhaps his mother, when he was two or three, and she'd be slipping his pajama top over his head, getting him ready for bed. He never connected Raoul's version of the phrase with his mom's until later, when he'd be furiously scribbling down notes of everything that happened.

Pulling out the largest gun Peter had ever seen, perhaps the largest gun ever made, the handgun not yet invented, Raoul reached at arm's length and pressed its tip hard between Peter's eyes. He repeated himself.

"Fucking arms up. Now. I don't have all fucking day."

His tone beat home the fact that he didn't like repeating himself.

Raising his arms over his head, Peter held his breath while Raoul patted him down, looking for the mysterious wire that would frame him for untold crimes.

"I'm not wearing—"

"Shut up," Raoul said. Then, nodding to himself, content that he wasn't being recorded, "You can put your arms down."

Peter did as he was told.

"Now, what's in the bag?"

Peter went to open it, but was stopped by one of the big man's hands pulling the messenger bag from his grasp.

"Uh-uh-uh. I'll do that."

Peeling back its top, he pulled out a notepad, a book on drug addiction, and Peter's stiletto letter opener.

Holding the blade out with one hand for Peter to see, his pistol with the other, Raoul laughed heartily as if playing some deranged game of Rock, Paper, Scissors.

"Bullet beats knife."

And he laughed again. Tossing Peter's belongings back into the leather bag, then dropping the bag to the floor by Peter's feet. He gave the writer a once-over, then muttered, "Shit, man, relax. I'm just fucking with you," before yelling out, "Lucinda! Beer!"

Raoul turned back to Peter then. "Have a seat."

The sofa was black leather and probably cost as much as the New York Times Magazine *designer swag in Halli-*

well's flat, but this piece of furniture was worth the price. It was like sinking back into the womb. It held you gently, perhaps even a little sensually. Raoul liked his comfort.

Awash in the pleasure of the sectional, Peter looked up suddenly to see Lucinda approach. Petite and wearing not much at all, she was fresh fruit, and deadly. China white with flowing dark brown hair, and a way with her green eyes that needed to be illegal.

That probably was illegal.

She carried out two ice-cold Stellas, placing them down on the pristine oak coffee table at Peter's knee, bending before him in a way that made him know he should look away, but over which he was powerless to resist.

Lucinda caught his stare. "Would you like anything else?" she asked, her voice fragile and curious.

Peter turned away, catching the look on Raoul's face, Raoul who'd been staring at him all along. He grinned like the lights of Broadway.

"Get out of here," Raoul said.

Lucinda scattered.

Picking up one of the beers, Raoul handed it to Peter, suddenly speaking as if he were his new best friend. Sounding, oddly enough, Peter thought, like a used-car salesman.

"You like that, huh?" Raoul said, staring him down. "You want a taste."

It was Peter who turned away first, not answering. He looked over toward the hallway into which Lucinda disappeared. It wasn't about him liking the girl. Or wanting her. What Peter wanted was in her head. Her reasons. The why and where and how of what she did. Of how she ended up in this basement apartment in Alphabet City. Of how she became a whore, maybe a drug addict. Of the turns that took her on a trip to hell, instead of to the mall, or the high school *dance, or Thanksgiving dinner with her brothers and sisters in a big white house in some small Connecticut town.*

Everything had changed.

His entire concept out the window.

He realized right at that moment that she was why he was here.

Lucinda *was the book.*

So much more than Raoul, who'd become the stereotype, the cowboy pimp to the point of no return. Beyond being saved, he'd remember little of how he got there. As far as Raoul was concerned, he gave it no thought. He'd always been a professional piece of shit.

Lucinda, on the other hand, regretted the decisions that brought her here, that sank her deeper, every day of her life.

Peter was sure of it.

So sure he'd bet his life.

So sure, he thought, another laugh bringing him back, making him turn to stare at Raoul, who was reading his interest in Lucinda in all the wrong ways.

"Nothing like fresh meat to take the edge off a hard day," the piece of shit said.

Lucinda

"How did you start?"

"Saw it on Oprah."

They were in a small French pastry shop on Spring Street, just off Lafayette. It was where he'd arranged with Raoul for them to meet. He was getting a "professional discount," as her pimp called it. Five hundred for two hours of her time, half off the normal price for a girl of her age and ability.

She was a little surprised at first when Peter told her he just wanted to talk.

"Oh, talk first and then . . ." Lucinda said, with a suggestive batting of her eyes.

"No," Peter explained. "Just talk."

"About?"

"You," he told her.

Peter laughed at her response.

"No, really, Oprah," she explained. "Like, these three girls were talking about all this money they were making. And even though they said they regretted it and stuff, I could tell—they missed it. They missed the money. The attention. I mean, it's just sex, right?"

She was dressed in jeans and a T-shirt. Something any other girl her age would wear. Peter's request, when Raoul asked. "You want her to look young," he had said.

"I want her to blend into the crowd" was Peter's response.

"What was it like the first time?" he asked, jotting down notes as she sipped French lemonade and nibbled on a chocolate croissant.

"Fun," she said.

He shot her a look.

"No, really," she said. "I answered this ad in the Village Voice *from a"—she hooked her fingers like quotation marks—"'generous gentleman seeking adventurous young women who like the finer things in life.'" She shrugged. "He was nice, really knew what he was doing. I mean, y'know, in bed. It never felt that good before." She looked down at the pastry, pulling it apart with her fingers. When she looked back up she was blushing, almost as if a blush were expected. "He gave me a thousand dollars for the two hours, and said he wanted to see me every week." Another shrug. "I mean, it was like a no-brainer, right?"*

"I guess," Peter said. Then: "How long ago was this?"

A shrug. "Three years."

"How old were you that first time?"

"Thirteen," she said, taking a sip of her lemonade.

They met one other time. Same place. Same discount. But when Peter called to set up a third meeting, Raoul laid down his law.

"I don't rent my bitches out to talk," he explained.

Peter didn't speak to Lucinda again for almost two years. But for now he had enough for Angel.

PART THREE

Angel

"Angel, you little slut!"

Kelly, her best friend since second grade, grinned like a jackrabbit. She stared in wide-eyed disbelief as Angel shrugged it off as no big deal, knowing full well that to Kelly it was a very big deal.

"It was your first date," Kelly said.

True enough. Saturday night of pizza and a movie with a sophomore, and freshman Angel was bored out of her mind. All she could think about was what she'd done for the first time with Richard the night before.

Cocaine.

She was frightened at first. But Richard sucked on the tip of his index finger, dipped it into the white powder, then rubbed it on her gums. She was shaking when his finger went back for more, then this time found its way between her legs.

It was the first time she hadn't made it home before her eleven p.m. curfew. And she was sure she'd be grounded. But her mom was out with friends, and never even asked what time Angel got home.

At the end of their time together, as Richard paid for his

pleasure, he told Angel that a friend of his would be joining them next week. That he wanted to watch her make love to another man. He didn't ask her if that was okay; he was paying for it to be.

"Will there be more of this?" she asked, doing another line.

"An endless supply," Richard promised.

That was all she could think about as her date blabbered on about video games and skateboards and some stupid show on MTV.

So when the check was split, and it came time for the movie, Angel was the one who suggested they do something else.

"Wanna play some video games?" he suggested.

That wasn't what Angel had in mind. She explained that she'd never seen one up close before, and if he showed her his, she'd put it in her mouth. The sophomore lasted for all of thirty seconds, and never spoke for the rest of the night. Which was fine with Angel.

"I like quiet," she told him afterward.

He wasn't a stupid boy.

Recounting the story to her best friend, she left out the part about Richard, his friend, about the coke, and instead shrugged her experience with the sophomore off as wanting to see what all the fuss was about.

Kelly feigned shock, then laughed, then demanded every detail.

Angel was quick to oblige, exaggerating a little, making a face about the taste, mimicking the sounds he made at that most climactic moment.

"Sounds like a seal honking," Kelly said.

"Sort of," Angel said.

"Are you going to see him again?"

"Why not?" Angel said.

The inept boy was a good cover. Someone she could intro-duce to her mom, use as an excuse to get out of the house dur-ing the week. The nice things she'd been wanting to buy for herself could be gifts, or borrowed from her new beau.

Angel blushed as Kelly started teasing, "Angel's got a boyfriend. Angel's got a boyfriend."

But that blush had nothing to do with the sophomore, and everything to do with how much easier he would make it for her to see more of Richard and experience whatever it was he had in mind.

Dina and Halliwell

It was easier than she expected.

Proof, in her mind, at least, that *Angel* was more fact than fiction. The ad was still running, exactly as transcribed in his notebook, down to the phone number, both altered just slightly in the novel. She called; he answered on the second ring. She lied about her age; he made an appointment. But being petite and so fair skinned, she could easily pass for a sixteen-year-old.

One who desired the finer things in life.

He answered the door, a cellular phone pressed to his face. The phone was black and sleek and seemed a natural extension of his left hand, as if the cuff of his jacket had been tailored to take the phone into account.

"Meet me halfway and we've got a deal," Jeffrey Halliwell said, lowering the phone only slightly from his face, waiting for his visitor to speak.

"Mr. Halliwell?" she said, staring up into his eyes.

"You must be Dina," he said, appraising her like a stock portfolio.

She nodded demurely.

"Got to go," he barked into the phone, snapping it shut, slipping it into his jacket pocket, then smiling. "You're right on time."

"Do you like wine?" he asked, handing her a glass.

"I can learn to," she said, taking a sip.

"Good answer," he said, pouring himself one, holding it up to the light for inspection. "This is a 1964 Palmer Bordeaux."

"It's older than me," she said, a smile to play up *What a silly thing to say.*

"A lot older," he said, buying into the teenage charm.

Dina took another sip.

"May I ask you a question?" she said.

"Depends on the question," he replied.

She bit down coyly on her bottom lip. "I have two, actually." A short pause as she looked away, feigning embarrassment. "How generous are you?"

Halliwell removed a roll of crisp one-hundred-dollar bills from his pocket and, counting out twenty-five, pressed them into her free hand. Dina pretended the money excited her. Taking a deep breath, as if lost, she dropped the bills into her purse.

"Satisfactory answer?" he asked.

Nodding, placing her glass of wine down on the nearest surface, Dina moved closer. She ran a hand down the front of his shirt, tugging playfully on a middle button.

"And how adventurous do you expect me to be?"

"I never want to hear you say the word *no,*" he told her.

As a first response she leaned up to kiss him.

"Another good answer," he said, pulling her close,

kissing her again, holding her in a tight embrace, until his eyes opened suddenly in a hard blink.

Halliwell gasped; something was very wrong. He tried to speak, but only a click of sorts escaped his lips.

Taking a rough step back, his hand slamming down on the closest table, knocking the bottle of Bordeaux to the floor, he looked down at the handle protruding from the chest. Silver, a little tarnished, with worn swirls and the initials P.R.

Dina gave the handle a good tug and pulled the long blade free, taking with it a streak of Halliwell's blood.

"It's not even in my vocabulary," she said, her voice dark, as she stepped away, watching Halliwell drop to his knees, just as she dropped Peter's stiletto discreetly into her purse atop the hundred-dollar bills.

She finally understood his addiction to playing God. *What a way to get off,* she thought, *deciding who lives and who dies in the world of your own making.*

How Long?

The red-and-blue flashing lights seemed foreign on the quiet tree-lined block. Foreign and violent and sur-real—*this can't be happening to me.* Domestic terrorism against the sandman and all his pharmaceuticals just wanting to help us all to a good night's sleep.

They certainly added some much needed color to Jeffrey Halliwell's living room. A light show through the floor-to-ceiling living room windows.

Looking as if she hadn't slept through a night in a very long while, Detective Paula Rossi knelt beside the sheet-covered corpse, the white cotton a reflector for the turbulence of the lights, the blood soaking through more welcoming, as if pulling in an old friend. A bottle of spilled wine adding to the morose rainbow.

Rossi wondered what it felt like for a blade to slice into your heart. Not figuratively. Figuratively she knew. The literal, that was what she was curious about. Was there a difference? Was it more painful, or less? It certainly was a lot messier. And a lot quicker as well.

That was a plus.

Falling into the hypnotic rhythm of the red-blue-red-blue, she wondered what this son of a bitch had done to deserve it. Not that she was placing blame on the victim, but so few were ever innocent. So many deserved exactly what they received. Some deserved worse and walked free.

Victims held endless possibilities.

Or maybe she'd just been at the job a few years, a few corpses too long.

How long? That was the real question.

—had Halliwell been lying here?

Two to three hours, give or take. Until a neighbor walking her dog noticed his door wide-open.

—had his killer been planning the attack?

Or was it a random break-in, spawned by a vicious streak, a depressed lifetime?

—would they remain free?

Shrugging to the questions playing in her head, Rossi rose on creaky knees, thinking that the only question she wanted an answer to was, How long before she could light up again?

The answer to that one was easy.

Too long.

Taking in the rest of his pad. That was the only word for it, at least in her mind: *Miami Vice* on a Donald Trump budget. The ultimate bachelor digs, all black leather and tinted glass, so stuck in the eighties, Rossi half expected the best of Duran Duran to be playing on a never-ending loop.

She stood before an original Nagel, signed to Halliwell, as if he were a friend, instead of a rich devotee, wondering what the piece had set its owner back. A raven-haired, red-lipped beauty, wearing huge gold hoops, her ripped gray sweatshirt falling off one shoulder, breast exposed. A *Flashdance* fantasy.

"Get over it already," Rossi muttered.

Walking down a hallway lined with questionable trophies, she stepped into the master bedroom suite. Sitting on the edge of the California king–size bed, she pulled open the top night table drawer, poking at its contents with the tip of a ballpoint pen.

Pharmacy neat, square clear-plastic parcels of pills and other highs and lows: X, coke, GHB, speed, Vicodin, Adderall, and a small neatly packed bag of weed.

The fruits of Halliwell's labor.

The desk was black glass and pristine. Free even of fingerprints and dust, as if in an airtight museum display, or as though Halliwell had none and dust wouldn't dare.

Rossi found Halliwell's Palm Pilot pulled into a docking station on the desk just off to the side of Halliwell's computer monitor, a flat panel that was at least the size of the TV in her living room.

She was reluctant to pick it up at first. To put a smudge on its gleaming silver surface. But cleanliness was never really her style, godliness notwithstanding. Fingerprints and dust were natural, beautiful; at least, that was what she willed herself to believe every time she entered her one-bedroom walk-up in Astoria.

Holding down the power button, the color screen warming to life, the lack of password protection making it easy. Rossi scrolled through Halliwell's address book, the names listed alphabetically, the phone numbers next, a small icon to identify cellular versus home versus work numbers.

Hitting the Ls, she found the number for Mike Levine, the name ringing some sort of foreign bell, not immediately recognizable, but familiar. But certainly not as familiar as who was waiting for her six letters down.

"Son of a bitch," she muttered, turning off the Palm and bagging it as evidence.

Dina and Peter

She could read it now.

Wide-awake and with a cup of coffee in hand, Dina sat sideways on the oversize windowsill behind her sofa, leaning back against the cold of the painted wall, crooking her left leg up toward the glass, her knee tapping against it, comfortable.

She wore the *Angel* T-shirt. Also comfortable—and comforting, in that it smelled like Peter, at least in her mind. It reminded her of his office, of the secret chamber where the mystical ingredients of Angel's birth were kept, like pieces of Christ's cross in the altar of a Catholic church.

Lifting the manuscript onto her lap, she stared at the title page, reading the name out loud. She wondered where the title came from. She once read in a short *Entertainment Weekly* interview with Peter that the name Angel came from the Jimi Hendrix song. That he would play the track on an almost endless repeat when writing, and that he'd never been able to listen to it again since.

Though it was a good quote, deep down Dina believed Peter was covering for someone real. Someone whose identity would never be known. Would never be acknowledged. A real Angel.

When she finished this sequel, she would do a Google search to see if there was a song called "It's a Wonderful Lie" that Peter would never again listen to either.

Peter sat back in his tension-relieving chair, rocking back, far back, leaning at that edge of falling over backward. He'd done that before, a number of times. Voiding out the warning label that he was sure probably came with the chair—such labels seemed to come with everything except that which we really needed warning of—hardly the Czechoslovakian chiropractor's intent. Always alone. Always feeling ridiculous afterward. Never really on purpose.

Staring at the blank computer screen, the words not forming, just the jumble of letters on the keyboard, making about as much sense as if you tried to pronounce them out loud.

Making no sense at all.

Hooking a foot against the edge of his desk, he realized he wanted to know what it felt like, just once, without the surprise, without the twinge of dumb-ass guilt.

He was far enough back. So, just the slightest push. A shove off. Like jumping.

Backward.

The computer falling away, the Virgin Mary with it, just the eternal white of the ceiling coming into view as he landed, a soft thud, laughing, wishing it were all this easy.

*   *   *

She needed something stiff.

Pages in hand, Dina jumped over the words, her jaw clenching, annoyed, the smile long gone. Pacing into the kitchen, slamming the empty coffee cup into the sink, a few bottles of relief in a cabinet overhead, a wet bar of sorts. Hauling down the Cointreau and a glass to go with it. A handful of ice. A splash. She let it swirl around a little, but there wasn't time for it to cool. The next shot or the one after that she'd sip. Right now she needed the edge off.

"No, no, no, no," she hollered.

Absentmindedly he played with the handcuffs, opening and closing them against his thigh. Then typing finally. Wanted to at least feel the bounce of his fingertips against the keyboard. He always typed to a rhythm. Not a song, even if one were playing. Just a beat. A little syncopation. It was easy at the moment, five letters, then four, five letters, then four.

Over and over again. Until there seemed nothing else he needed to write.

A-N-G-E-L, he typed.

Then: D-I-N-A.

His hands moved faster and faster on the keys, until the letters blended together, and new words were formed, a new never-ending name, a gibberish tribute to how she'd taken over his life.

Dina hit the last page with a vengeance. Wanting the thing to just be over and done with. Like abuse. Like rape.

"You can't fucking do this," she screamed.

Disconnected

Her voice sounded as if it were coming from another lifetime.

"Hey, honey," Julianna said. "Have a good day writing?"

Peter stared at his wife from his vantage point on the couch. He held a drink in hand, not coffee, something stronger. Not to take the edge off, but to dull the pain. It had been one of those sorts of writing days.

He shook the glass just enough for the ice to clink.

"Oh," Julianna said.

He knew she understood that a good day did not equal drinking alone. A good day was euphoric. A good day was smiles. A good day was pizza at Grimaldi's in Brooklyn, and a walk by the waterfront taking in the Manhattan skyline.

She looked as if she were about to say something else, perhaps offer condolences, when the phone rang. The wireless handset rattling on the coffee table to its own bile-producing *skreak*.

"If it's Verizon," Julianna said, stepping back into the kitchen, "give them my love."

Glaring at the phone. Willing it to stop. To never ring again. He knew. If not this call, then the one after or the one after that. Eventually it would be Dina on the other end of the line, telling him she'd finished the book.

Leaning forward with a few too many creaks for a man of his age, Peter placed the now-empty-except-for-ice glass onto the table and picked up the phone. Pressing the TALK button, he brought the receiver to his ear. "Hello," he said.

Silence for a beat, then: "You made her weak."

"What?" he asked, not sure, not understanding the tone, the anger, not recognizing the voice or the rage. "Who is this?"

"You know very fucking well who this is," she yelled.

Yes, now he did. Peter could picture her. Her face twisted in some sort of Munchian nightmare.

"You made her weak."

Julianna popped her head back into the room. "Hungry?" she asked.

Holding up a finger as if to say, *One minute*, Peter ended the call. "I'm not interested," he said.

He could hear her yell, "Don't you dare hang up on me!" as he pressed the END button and cut the connection.

"Who was that?" Julianna asked.

"No one," he said, slapping the back of the receiver a few times hard against his open palm.

The ringer startled him.

"Looks like no one is calling back," she said.

He punched the TALK button.

"Look," he snapped, "I don't know how you fucking got this number . . ."

"It was on your title page, genius," she said.

". . . but don't ever call here again."

She managed to get out, "You afraid the little wife will find out what's—" before he hung up on her again, this time slamming the phone onto the coffee table, once, then again, harder the second time. Combing his hair back with his fingers to the point of pain.

"What's going on?" Julianna asked.

She was standing right beside him now. So near he was afraid to look up. Afraid that she might recognize betrayal at such close quarters.

It took a moment for Peter to come up with a lie. And when he did, he still couldn't look at her.

"She . . ."

"Who?"

He picked up the receiver again, squeezing the life out of it, his thumbnail flicking the tiny ringer button to the OFF position.

". . . was screaming at me."

He placed it carefully back down, facedown, the caller ID covered. So many warnings of the danger to come in this digital age.

"What are you talking about?"

"About the new book."

"Your new book?"

He wondered if it was *his* anymore. If anything was. Or had ownership all been transferred because of that one slip with Dina? She acquired his life, and all sense of Peter ceased to exist.

"Yes," he said, looking up finally, just as she sat down beside him.

"I don't understand."

"I wanted an outside opinion," Peter explained. "So, I"—a shrug, another beat in which to think—"found a readers' group online, fans of the first book. I sent out an e-mail to the members asking if anyone might be interested in a blind read of the sequel. I exchanged e-mails with everyone who replied, and well, she seemed"—he shrugged—"the brightest."

"Seems like a psycho to me."

"Yeah, well. Live and learn," he said. "She's been calling like that for a few days now. I didn't want to tell you because I didn't want you to worry, or think that something was going on."

"How'd she get our number?"

"My best guess," he said, "there's a registry of every Web address in the world with contact info, name, address, phone, for the owner of every URL." He remembered such a thing as a plot point for an episode of *Law & Order*.

"And all of our info's there?"

"Not anymore. I changed it. I put in the fax number instead. The address of the publishing house."

"But still," Julianna said, the lie taking root.

Dina

She had forgotten about the T-shirt.

Catching her reflection in the full-length mirror on her bedroom closet door. The face of Angel staring back, mocking her for her weakness, laughing at the way Peter had treated her, dismissive to the point of abuse because of the lack of respect he had shown in those new words.

But even Angel couldn't think of her like that. Grabbing the neck of the cotton T-shirt, she ripped it open right down the middle, falling to her knees in front of the mirror, tearing the shirt now from her body, tearing her skin as well. She shredded the shirt at every seam, destroying the face of Angel, as he had destroyed her memory with words. Making cotton confetti until her nails ripped, her fingertips bled, until the tears and snot and blood clotted into a twisted cotton ball that no one could ever recognize.

The Sunday Times

It was a Sunday ritual, one that Groucho seemed to look forward to perhaps even more than Peter. The dog seemed to have some sort of internal calendar. An alarm of sorts that went off every seven days. He sat by the side of their bed now, Peter's side, leash in mouth, a small whine. Only loud enough to wake Peter, who slit an eye open, focusing on the digital readout of that old phone/clock radio. Seven thirty. He shot the dog a look. Like clockwork.

The headline grabbed his attention. Familiar, yet shocking. Always shocking when someone you knew died. More so if it was murder. Glancing down at the waist-high stack of the Sunday *New York Post*. The headline bold: "West Village Slaughter."

The photo of "restaurateur" Jeffrey Halliwell not at all flattering. A drunken late-night-party shot. Eyes glazed, lips too numb even to snarl. The side of some young woman's face pressed against his. But even in black and white it showed his true colors.

"Want me to get you a chair?" the gargle of a voice asked. "So you can be more comfortable?"

The gargle was sarcastic.

Peter looked up catching the glare of the guy running the newsstand, the Yankees cap framing his white-whiskered face, sweatshirt with rolled-up sleeves, covered by an old *New York Times* apron, the side of its pockets ripped. The guy was annoyed. He was a New Yorker.

"Sorry," Peter said.

"This ain't a library."

"I know, I, ah . . ."

He picked up the *Post*, as well as the *Times* and the *Daily News*, then handed over the cash.

"Spacing out," Peter said. "Y'know."

"Sure thing," he replied, rolling his eyes, handing back some change.

Peter tugged on Groucho's leash.

"C'mon, boy," he said, the seven pounds of newsprint jammed under one arm.

Stepping away, Peter caught the first part of the newspaper guy's exchange with his next customer.

"City's fucking filled with them," he said.

Acknowledgments

She was waiting on his front stoop. Smoking a cigarette, pinching the filter between her index finger and thumb, cupping the fag as if to protect if from the elements. An ex-partner/ex-lover had once told her she smoked like a man. She replied that he fucked like a girl.

That was the end of that.

Stubbing it out the moment he was close enough to be bothered, she stood, brushing away what little dirt her dark suit might have latched onto from the concrete.

"Peter," she said.

"Detective Rossi," he said. "This is a surprise. I hope it's a social call."

"Not completely," she said.

"Not completely?" he repeated as a question.

She changed the subject. "How've you been?"

"Hanging in there," he said, seeming not to notice. "You, um, want to come up?"

"No, maybe next time. This'll only take a minute. I'm working the Jeffrey Halliwell murder."

He tapped the stack of papers under his arm. "Just heard about that."

"You knew him, right?"

"Talked to him once."

"Only once?"

"Yeah. That was enough. Why?"

"I found your name in the address book of his Palm Pilot."

Peter said nothing.

She hastened a guess. "Was he one of your sources for *Angel*?"

"Maybe."

"Just maybe?"

"Yeah, he was a source," he said reluctantly.

"Did you meet any of his"—she searched for the least incriminating word, though the way she pronounced it probably didn't help—"associates?"

"Someone who'd want him dead?" Peter asked.

"That would be useful."

"No, Detective," he said, smiling.

"How did he help?" she asked. "If you don't mind my asking."

"And if I do?"

"Tell me anyway."

"He helped me find Angel," Peter said.

"That's pretty major, wouldn't you say? Considering I don't remember seeing his name on the acknowledgments page."

"I don't remember seeing yours," Peter replied. "Some people prefer to remain anonymous."

She nodded, understanding that that was often the best way to be. Anonymous, invisible, bulletproof, plain. "How'd you meet him?"

"He's a friend of my agent, Mike Levine."

"Levine's your agent?" she asked. "I knew that name sounded familiar. You acknowledged him, right?"

"Yeah, of course. I could have never gotten the book published without him. Why?"

"His name's on the Palm Pilot too."

"I'm sure that address book has a pretty long list of names."

Nodding, Rossi pulled a fresh cigarette from a now stale pack, and lit up as she walked away.

"Never ending," she said.

Happiness

It was serene, and not completely real. More like a snapshot of happiness. Like a commercial that used to run on the local New York stations, the picture-perfect family and their addiction to the Sunday *Times*.

The sections spread out, a few immediately tossed into the recycle bin, everyone with their favorite. Peter perused the book reviews from the corner of the sofa, his other sections of choice—Arts and Leisure and the *Magazine*—awaiting his attention on the end table. Julianna devoured "The Week in Review" from the dining room table—the living room table really, the only table. Sitting at her little homework desk, Kimberly looked at the photos in the travel section, picking out what appeared to be the perfect beach for their next vacation. Even Groucho, in repose in front of the family TV, rested front paws atop the society page spread out on the well-worn Oriental. He nibbled at a corner of the paper, bored.

But on this Sunday there was an uneasy quiet. Peter just sort of flipped the pages, not checking as he once did the names atop the best-seller lists, the names he'd most like to, most likely, dethrone. Even the newsprint didn't stick to his fingers. And reading the *New York Times* without blackened fingertips was just not reading the *New York Times* at all.

"Are you okay, Daddy?" Kimberly asked, obviously bored with the travel editor's choice of photos in this week's edition.

Peter looked over first at his wife. Her unspoken response echoed their daughter's question. Nodding, Peter looked over at Kimberly and motioned for her to come sit next to him on the sofa.

"Daddy's trying to finish up his new book," he said, "so . . . my mind is . . ."

"Confused?" the little girl offered up.

"That's the nice way of putting it," Julianna said, standing, joining the rest of her family on the sofa.

"Sort of," Peter said. "Let's just say I'm distracted."

Kimberly appraised her father, her brow crinkled well beyond her years.

"When are you gonna be finished?" she asked.

"Real soon, pumpkin," he said.

"But like when?" she persisted.

"You want a date?" he said.

"You always were good with deadlines," Julianna said.

Peter liked deadlines. Loved them back in his reporting days. Even those self-imposed. They gave his otherwise unordered existence structure. They added the light to the end of the tunnel when working on a story . . . or a novel. A tunnel that otherwise would be black and eternal, like a journey to the center of the earth. Like a road trip to hell.

"Okay, um . . ." he said, giving it some thought, a

mental calculation of how many chapters needed to be tweaked, the details, the story arches that could use a quick touch-up, the final read-through to catch all those typos. He scratched out some numbers in the margins of the *Book Review*, twisting up his mouth in mock contemplation, making Kimberly laugh.

"Okay, according to my scientific calculations . . ." he said.

"Scientific?" Julianna said.

"Daddy, you're being silly."

He remained serious, or as serious as possible, considering the situation. "I think we could expect an end to this craziness next Friday."

"That soon?" Julianna asked, honestly surprised.

Peter nodded. "I'm almost done. Just a couple of chapters need work."

"And you'll be ready to let her go?" Julianna asked.

"Yes," he said matter-of-factly.

"You promise, Daddy?"

"I promise, pumpkin," Peter replied.

He was ready to let her go.

Blink

Blink.

Alone now, in front of the computer. His hands quiet. The rage, the rush his fingertips had been feeling, the urge to touch their names, and only their names, in this way, his way, having long since passed. Peter stared at the muted grays surrounding the stark white of his computer screen, a frame, the blank page, word processor style.

Blink.

He remembered the phone, its ringer off. Reaching over, picking up the handset, his thumb caressing the TALK button, as if the softest touch could turn it on. Wondering if she'd called again, he pressed the back arrow on the caller ID. Nothing recent. Even her last call was not registering. Perhaps he had answered too quickly. Perhaps her rage had frightened this technology.

Flipping the ringer back on, he placed the phone down by his keyboard, to the left of it. He always answered the phone with his left hand. He could answer it quicker this way. If she called again.

Blink.
The nausea washed over him.

People this time.

Faces he had never seen, crouching low, as if about to be attacked. The fear so goddamn real, tears welling from their bowels, faces twisted in that momentary deceit that we are all about to die. They moved, each of them on their own stilted stumps, *backward* in time from the attack position, attack mode, straightening, relaxing, never expecting what was about to happen.

Waiting now only for the light to change.

Revocation

With no light behind her, the Virgin Mary became a reflecting pool for the glow off his monitor. She was sexier in this light. Bar light almost. *The end of the night, the edge long gone, and you've been sitting next to me on this bar stool for far too long. He ain't showing, honey. You've been stood up again.*

The knock was too soft for Peter to hear. Her voice as well.

"I knew you were working and didn't want to bother you, so Kimberly and I grabbed pizza. Are you hungry?"

He was starving. "What time is it?" he asked.

"Almost eight," she replied. "Would you like me to make you something?"

Anything.

"I think you could maybe use a break."

"Yeah," he said, breathing deeply, turning finally to face her. He wanted to tell her, to explain, to beg forgiveness. To cry.

"A break sounds good."

What would he do if she left?

"What, baby?" she said. "You look as if you want to say something."

What would he do without her?

"I'm . . . just . . ."

The ringing of the phone shot the rest of his sentence dead.

Turning, snatching the receiver off the desktop, he barked, "Hello?" looking confused as the ringing continued, catching Julianna's look, as they both turned.

The fax machine, over on the other side of the printer. Hardly used, but programmed nonetheless to answer after the second ring. Its beep was followed by a hollow sucking sound as a sheet of paper was pulled into the machine.

Standing, Peter leaned forward, worried as to what might be coming. Feeling Julianna by his side, he watched the answer as it inched out of the machine.

"What the . . . ?"

The fax was on Peter's own letterhead. A short missive to his agent.

" 'As of today,' " Julianna read out loud from the fax, " 'I revoke the authority of Mike Levine to act on my behalf as an agent throughout the world.' "

She shot Peter a concerned look as he pulled the paper from the machine, examining what Mike had written at the bottom of the missive.

The letters, big, black, all blocky and bold.

FUCK YOU!

The Local

He was frightened by the subway.

Not the cars themselves, or the stench of the underground. Not by the creatures he believed walked the tunnels at night, zombies with half-eaten faces who pressed their foreheads to the windows just long enough to grab your attention, to make you think perhaps you were crazed, except for the smear of blood left against the window. Not by the riders, the sardines, crammed but unable to touch, to feel, afraid to feel. The avoidance of vacant eyes.

But by the rush forward, the indeterminate speed, the whoosh, smack, race against the other trains.

What if it never stopped? What if it couldn't stop? Would anyone even notice?

He rode the number six train from Astor Place to Fifty-ninth Street. He preferred the local, never understood the riders who took the six to Union Square, then hopped the number four express two stops up to Fifty-ninth. *Pick a car and stick with it,* he thought.

Peter never rode the express.

*   *   *

"You're not man enough to tell me to my face?"

Anger twisting his face, Mike Levine glared out the floor-to-ceiling windows in his penthouse living room. Forty-eight floors up, a view to die for. It was the view from Richard's apartment in *Angel*. Peter couldn't make it up any better than this.

"I've been with you since your first short story," Mike said, his voice shaking with anger. "I thought we were friends."

Peter sat on the sofa reading the letter. His letterhead. His signature. But not his words.

"I didn't send this," he said.

"Then who did?" Mike asked.

"I have an idea, but I don't think you'll believe me."

Mike turned back to face him. Perhaps it was the sincerity with which Peter stared back, but he softened. He seemed as if he wanted to believe his friend.

"Try me," Mike said.

They were out on the deck. Mike leaned against the railing. Peter stood back, close to the building, touching the outside wall as if to make sure it was there.

"Christ, Peter!" he said. "You don't let me read it, but you show it to some bimbo you're banging." He shook his head, drumming his fingers against the rail. "What the fuck were you thinking?"

"It was just a blow job," Peter answered quietly.

"What?"

"Just a blow job," he replied. "That's all it was."

"And you couldn't say no?" Mike asked, turning back to look at him, adding quickly, in some frank conspiratorial tone that twisted Peter's stomach into knots, "Not like I could ever say no."

"I was drunk."

"Great defense."

"She's my biggest fan."

"Ever better!"

"It gets worse," Peter said. "She called the other night."

"Your apartment?"

Peter nodded. "Screaming at me about the manuscript." He clenched his eyes shut and pictured Julianna. "What am I gonna do?"

Shaking his head, Mike walked back inside.

Peter caught the look on his face as he passed. If Mike were a doctor, the diagnosis would have been terminal.

"I've known my share of crazy broads," he said.

"What's that supposed to mean?" Peter asked, turning, following him back inside.

"You might have only gotten a blow job in Madison," Mike said, "but now you're about to get fucked."

Reassurance

She was sitting at the table when he got home. Legal documents laid out before her like a buttery spread. Pen in hand, holding it like a smoke. But not a Mont-blanc, or something befitting her position, just a cheap plastic ballpoint, a dozen for a dollar twenty-nine at the local office superstore. No guilt in gnawing on the ends, or losing a cap to Groucho, who'd treat it likewise as the world's smallest chew toy.

"When were you going to tell me?" she asked, before he even made it into the room. "About firing Mike?" In case there was any confusion.

"I'm not firing Mike," he said.

"But that letter . . . ?"

He pulled out the chair kitty-corner to where she was sitting, he leaned close, his elbows on the table.

"It was a mistake."

All a mistake, he thought. The biggest fucking mistake of his life.

"How do you fax someone a letter by mistake?" she asked.

"When you told me he'd stopped by . . ."

"He was worried about you."

"I know, but . . ."

Peter shrugged, not able to complete the lie.

"I know how you get when you're finishing a book," she said. "You live in this little fantasy world, and you seem to forget about the real world, and the real people around you."

"I don't forget, Julianna," he said. "Never. Not for a minute."

Tears came to her eyes, and Peter knew, in that very instant, he could never tell her. She must never find out. That to break her heart was unforgivable, to make her cry his greatest sin.

"You and Kimberly are my world," he said sincerely. He'd die first.

"And Groucho?"

"And Groucho."

She nodded, sniffled, and hugged him dearly. He kissed her forehead.

"I love you so much," one of them said.

Hell

Number 571.

East Sixth Street.

A lot closer to Avenue B than A, a five-story walk-up made of brick the color of smoldering cinders.

Climbing the four stairs to the front door, one that had certainly seen more than its fair share of break-ins, Peter looked for apartment 5-B on the panel of door-bells, buzzers, really, linked to an intercom that he suspected didn't work. He realized then that he didn't know her last name.

Scanning down the apartment numbers, never expecting to see the name of the person living in 5-B to be Bailey. His character's last name in the book. A first initial of G, which made no sense, but still, he knew it was her. He knew it was Dina.

Wondering when it would stop, or how it would stop—he would *make* it stop—Peter thought twice about pressing the buzzer, and tried the door instead.

It wasn't even locked.

*   *   *

The stairwell smelled of sulfur. The paint on the walls peeling, the railings as stained and sticky as the stairs themselves. He could swear he heard pain as he passed the other apartment doors on his way up to the top floor. Torture, muffled moans, the tearing of flesh, or perhaps he just believed she deserved to reside in hell.

Her door was recently painted bright blue, Angel's favorite color. The numbers, 5-B, likewise new, a brushed aluminum, as if just purchased at some hardware store. Even the screws holding the numbers on seemed to have fresh metal scrapings on their heads.

He knocked twice.

After a beat, if that even—it was as if she knew he was coming, as if she were waiting for him—the door opened. Dina, barefoot, wearing loose-fitting jeans and an old tank top, stood glaring at him. She said not a word, but instead shook her head, then opened the door wider to let him enter, slamming it shut behind him in disgust.

The moment the lock clicked into place, Peter grabbed her by the throat and threw her up against the closest wall.

"What the hell do you think you're doing?" he yelled, holding her there, pressing his thumb into the soft flesh under her chin, realizing how breakable she was, how ultimately delicate, how he could end this with one tight squeeze. Maybe she had taught him about violent urges after all.

It took a moment for Dina to respond, but when she finally did, it was in a hoarse whisper, the words choked and a little bruised.

"Fuck me," she said.

Shaking his head as if he couldn't believe what he'd heard, Peter again slammed her hard against the wall.

Dina leaned up, bit his earlobe hard, and whispered, "Isn't it what you fantasize about when you're with your wife?"

His breathing ragged, Peter pushed her back, moving away, turning away, staring down hopelessly at the floor. How could she be so sure? he wondered.

How could he deny the truth?

"You're sick," he said, knowing he wasn't any better.

"You need me, Peter," she said, rubbing at her neck, touching what would probably become a bruise, seeming to get off on the pain he inflicted. "I complete you. I'm the part of you with balls."

She laughed, circling him now like a vulture.

"What, no comment?" She softened her approach just a bit. "You need me to finish this book. You know that. You can't get it right without me."

"I don't need you, Dina. I haven't been able to write one goddamn word since I met you."

"Because you can't stop thinking about how you want to fuck me? What you want to do to me?"

He could feel the rage and resentment eating away at his soul. He spit out the words: "You could say that."

"So do it," she said. "Set yourself free."

He shook his head, remembering Mike's warning about being fucked. "Stay out of my life," he said calmly.

Shaking her head, Dina laughed, an evil smirk twisting her face. "Or what?" she asked. "You'll have me arrested? That would look real good, especially to your wife."

Peter looked up, finally taking in her apartment. There was nothing even slightly off-kilter about it, nothing to warn a visitor as to the true nature of the beast inside. Just your average Pottery Barn catalog come to life, comfortable, a little girlish, on a budget. He spotted his manuscript on her coffee table.

"Did you write that letter to Mike?"

"Yes," she replied.

"Why?"

"To get your attention. To stop you before you destroyed me."

"You're *not* Angel!" Peter cried.

"I know more about her than you do," she said, suddenly quoting the book from memory, "'She put the lipstick on last, amused that it was always what would come off first, before even the most obvious stitch of clothing. On lips sometimes, or a cheek, or less likely a starched white collar.'"

"Those are *just* words," Peter yelled.

"'But usually, at least half the time, it found its way elsewhere, a marking, well-charted territory, a bright red macho cock-ring tattoo.'"

"Why are you doing this?"

"Why are you?"

Suddenly charged, fired up, Dina went to her sofa. She took a seat on the edge of the middle cushion. Something about the way she sat immediately distracted Peter. Her legs open, the tank low-cut and loose. But she wasn't trying to turn him on now; instead she leaned close to the coffee table and slapped open the manuscript.

"Angel was never weak," she said, her voice calm, as if arguing a valid point. "That's what made her special.

She started out as a happy, ballbusting girl who could get away with anything, and yeah, she made mistakes, a lot of them. But she freed herself from those mistakes and moved on." She shook her head. "But to have her return as some second-rate vigilante killing everyone who fucked her over . . ."

"She needs to make them pay," Peter said matter-of-factly.

"She already has by surviving," Dina argued. "Angel's strength lies in taking responsibility for her choices. Not in blaming others."

"That isn't enough. There needs to be blame."

"No. Peter. Please. You'll ruin it for everyone who ever loved this book, who at least for four hundred and twenty-two pages believed we all get a second chance."

"There are no second chances. You can't go through life living a lie. Perhaps *you* need to learn that. Angel certainly did."

"Angel or you?" she asked, catching him a little off guard. "I'm not married."

Kimberly and Dina

Kimberly sat alone on the steps to her school, making fountains with her eyes. Peter could not have possibly moved faster, the hapless horror of making her cry weighing on his conscience, weighing down his heart.

What the hell are you doing? he thought to himself, about himself. Probably his most frequent thought since Madison.

"Don't cry, pumpkin," he said, sweeping her into his arms, covering her forehead with kisses. "Daddy's here."

"I thought something had happened to you," she said, her voice heaving between immeasurable heartbreak and abandonment. "I was scared. I don't want anything to ever happen to you."

Peter shushed his daughter softly, his hand pressing gently against the back of her head, brushing her hair down, telling her, "I'll always be here for you. You know that. Daddy would never leave you."

After sniffling back a torrent of tears that could shred a heart, Kimberly, her jaw clenched, her cheeks swollen and flushed and trembling under the weight of such sadness, nodded finally.

But at least now in her father's arms she felt safe.

Dina watched them from across the street, trying to remember one moment from her childhood—desperate, happy, heartbreaking. She would have settled for anything. A lost smile on the corner of her mom's mouth. A giggle, a song, the bite of a crisp apple on a chilly fall day.

It was like that portion of her life had been erased, deleted, or worse, never written. Had it been so horrible that she had just blocked it out entirely?

Seeing the intensity with which the little girl gripped her father's neck saddened her greatly. She wished there were something in her own life that made her feel so secure, that gave her such joy, that actually made her glad to be alive.

Something at least more substantial than a book.

Kimberly played with toys in front of the TV. A favorite old doll, a Barbie knockoff with red hair and a suburban Goth costume of a black vinyl miniskirt and mesh tank top over a tight white shirt that had seen better years. But watching, Peter understood her devotion. It was like an old shirt, torn at the seams and faded to some color God never intended, but a war buddy, a partner, one you'd fight to the death for, never let go of.

Peter used to jokingly call the doll Hooker Barbie until Kimberly overheard the joke and asked what a hooker was.

"Yes, dear," Julianna had said at the time, enjoying

the moment, "what exactly is a hooker? I think we'd both like to know."

Peter never referred to the doll by that name again.

Watching Kimberly play now, he thought of how delicate she was, how delicate all of this was. So lost was Peter in a daze of how to forever protect her, shelter her, provide, that he didn't hear the buzzer ring, until—

"Daddy, there's someone at the door."

It took him a beat, hearing, realizing.

"I know," he said.

"Aren't you going to answer it?"

Holding her questioning glance for a beat, he stood finally, and as an answer walked to the intercom.

"Hello," he said, pressing the TALK button.

But there was no sound, no reply.

"Hello," he said again.

To let go.
Apologize.
Start over.
Hope for a second chance.
A reprieve.
Parole.
Make him realize.
How much he needed her.
Wanted her.
Loved her.
It was what she felt she needed to do at this point.

Peter stepped from the elevator and glanced down the hallway. Through the oval window in the first door he could see the foyer was empty except for the red-and-white flyer from a local Chinese joint that promised free delivery, no minimum purchase, which had been jammed into each of the twenty-four mailboxes.

A large manila envelope caught his attention the moment he opened the door. His name written in bold block letters, Sharpied the color black. Lifting it off the small table upon which such parcels were always left, he ripped open the envelope and pulled from it the manuscript to *It's a Wonderful Lie*.

Upon its title page had been written a note.

Peter, you are on the right track. I'm sorry for the way I behaved, it read.

It was signed, *Dina*.

Candy from Strangers

"That's all she wrote?" he asked.

Mike Levine stared at Peter with the look of a man waiting for the trigger to be pulled, or at least the punch line. But when no response came, almost no visible life from the eyes staring back at him, he added, "You okay?"

From across the vast expanse of his agent's desk, Peter nodded. He wasn't sure at this point if he felt relief or sadness, as if he somehow missed her already. He had no idea as to whether or not he was okay.

"She returned the manuscript, right?"

"Yeah," Peter replied, none too enthusiastically, thinking that the new novel felt real when it was in Dina's hands. What was a writer without a reader? "But what does it mean?"

"Easy," Mike replied. "The book is brilliant and she's sorry she ever called your house. She won't do it again."

"You make it sound . . . *easy*."

"It is. Stop trying to complicate everything in your life. Take the note at face value."

"I don't know that I trust her."

"She's female. Why would you?"

Peter nodded, but not for any of the reasons Mike would have suspected. His mistrust was not of the opposite sex, but of Dina specifically.

"I've known girls like this," Mike said. "One taste of your dick and they go a little crazy. Like it's theirs till death do you part." He sensed Peter's apprehension, and added, "It'll be fine."

"What if it's not? What if she—"

"Peter," Mike said, cutting him off. "Enough. You're sounding like a frazzled little girl. Just be a man, and learn from your mistake."

"What," Peter asked, knowing he was weak—weak-willed, weak-kneed—"don't accept blow jobs from strangers?"

"No," Mike replied, laughing. "Blow jobs are fine. Like candy. Take all you want."

"What then?"

"Your mistake was showing her the new book before you showed it to me. That's where you messed up big-time."

Nodding to himself, remembering the promised deadline, his promise to Kimberly, that this would all come to an end very soon, Peter stood. "You'll get it on Friday," he said.

"You're kidding," Mike said.

Peter shook his head. "I'm dead serious," he said.

Walking his client out of the office, Mike asked, "Are we still on for tonight?"

It took a beat for Peter to remember—what day,

what time, what plan. Perhaps it would do him good, a change of scenery, a little inspiration, or research, Mike style.

"Sure," he said, shaking his agent's hand good-bye. "Whatever."

Convert the Bastard

A gentlemen's club.

The name brought to mind mahogany-paneled rooms, brandy snifters, Cuban cigars, ascots, and talk of rugby. But as Peter followed Mike through the hallowed entrance of the establishment known as Scores, the notion that any patron had at any time within the boundaries of this club ever given rugby a thought, fleeting or otherwise, was ludicrous.

"Can't remember the last time I was here," Peter said.

"I can."

They passed a bouncer the size of a jet engine. Dressed in a tuxedo, his arms folded across his massive chest, he nodded at Mike.

"Good evening, Mr. Levine," he said, "welcome back."

Finding their way to a small round table barely the size of a dinner plate, Peter and Mike took a seat. The chair was a lot more comfortable than Peter would have imagined. Almost orthopedic. You could sit for hours. Perhaps that was the point. Many patrons did.

"Hi, Mike. Your usual?"

The voice came from a tall blonde, perfect in her proportions. She wore a bustier and a miniskirt, spiked heels, and just a touch of perfume. She knew how to lean over a table to get attention.

"Yes," Mike said, staring not into her eyes but down the front of her top, "and bring my friend here"—he thought for a beat—"a Stella?"

"Actually," Peter said, "make it a Cointreau on the rocks."

The drink took Mike's attention away from the waitress's perfect surgical specimens. He cocked an eyebrow. "Angel's pleasure. You're definitely in the zone."

Peter nodded, watching as the waitress squeezed Mike's shoulder as she walked past.

"Your home away from home?" Peter said.

Laughing ever so slightly, Mike turned, a creature onstage stealing his attention.

"Great atmosphere," Mike said. "Last time I was here . . ."

"Yesterday?"

"Last Wednesday," Mike answered, leaning a little closer to the stage, liking what he saw. "I was with Jeff Halliwell. He loved this place."

"Why does that not surprise me?" Peter said, remembering how everything about Halliwell turned his stomach.

"He was a good friend," Mike said.

"Guilt by association?" Peter said.

"Like a brother to me."

"Blood brothers."

Mike turned then, shooting Peter a harsh look. "Let's just say Jeff and I shared similar passions."

"Meaning?"

"A taste for the ladies."

"Ladies or girls?" Peter asked.

"No difference," Mike said, shaking his head, not bothering with further explanations, turning back instead, finding another dancer to steal his attention. If he noticed Peter's look of disapproval, there was no reaction, no concern.

"He hooked you up, didn't he?" Mike added.

Peter followed Jeffrey Halliwell as the millionaire walked to the curb and stepped up into a black Cadillac Escalade SUV. The vehicle was as overbearing as its driver.

"You want this book to sell?" Halliwell barked.

"Yeah, I guess that's part of it," Peter said.

"You want it to feel authentic?"

"Of course."

"Then take my advice," Halliwell said. "Experience a little of what Raoul has to offer. There's a big difference between actually knowing what you're writing about . . . and just taking someone's word for it."

"You have no idea what a young lady can do for your ego," Mike said.

"I don't need to know," Peter replied.

"You don't *want* to know, my friend. You're scared."

"And that's pathetic, isn't it?"

"Label it however you like," Mike replied, distracted.

Her stage name was Britney. She was long and lean as sin, with radiant blond hair and eyes stoned over with the manufactured look of desire.

"How about a private dance?" she whispered into Peter's ear.

"No," he said, "I can't—"

"Bullshit," Mike said, sounding only a fraction of how annoyed he probably was at this point. "You don't come here for the fucking drinks." He opened his wallet and slapped a small party of hundred-dollar bills into the girl's hand.

"Convert the bastard," he said.

The clothes, what little there were, melted off her like ice cream down the side of a cone on a hot summer day. Her body became liquid, engulfing Peter, drowning him in the dark, in the intoxicating smell of her sweat.

Clenching his eyes shut, wishing for it to all go away, he pictured a stoplight, changing, flashing, green to red, green to red, green to red. But something was wrong. Green was supposed to go to yellow, then to red. But there was no yellow, just green to red, green to red. And he realized it was in reverse.

Always in goddamn reverse.

Grabbing Britney, moving her away, Peter stood.

"I'm sorry," he said, feeling the room spin, the deceit take a choke hold. "I can't do this."

"Can I get you a cab, sir?"

Another jet engine whispering concern for a paying customer. So polite.

Leaning forward, letting the cold of the black marble wall cool his forehead, Peter waved off the question.

Then, turning away finally, he walked home.

Excuses

Her ashtray said she'd pulled an all-nighter.

Running Jeffrey Jonathan Halliwell's name through the system, looking for an arrest, a warrant, outstanding tickets, restraining orders, DUIs, coming up with none of the above.

What she did come up with surprised her.

Perhaps it was the small caches of drugs she'd discovered in almost every room of his town house, or the cash in his office safe. Two hundred forty-eight thousand dollars—a nice sum to have on hand in case of emergencies. Or the young escort who knocked on Halliwell's door the night after the murder, unaware that her sugar daddy was dead. Pushing her for information, Rossi discovered she was fifteen. She'd used his money, twenty-five hundred dollars for two hours, every other week like clockwork, to buy a laptop, an iPod, the latest cellular phone, and lots of clothes. She cried, begging the detective to please not tell her parents. Rossi let her go, no warning; she knew the girl would never listen. Victims rarely did.

Her surprise: Mr. Halliwell just didn't seem the victim type.

But it was a match nonetheless.

"Huh," Detective Rossi said, as she slipped another Camel out of the pack. Last one. Always a rush, always a little sadness. Though she liked the way the package felt in her hand when she crumpled it up. Helpless.

She lit up. The last public space where a person could smoke in peace. As long as you carried a shield. What fellow officer was going to arrest you for smoking while doing *this* job? Hell, she was surprised a carton of nonfiltereds and a flask of the hard stuff didn't come with the badge. To be a cop in New York City and not drink and smoke?

Make excuses, she thought, staring at the word *carjacking* on her computer monitor.

She started late, not in her teens or as an adolescent, as so many, as most. Twenty-four, in a bar alone for the first time in years, she'd just found husband number one in bed with her kid sister. The bartender offered her a smoke. He'd offer her a lot more by the time the night was over. She took him up on every last thing. Couldn't tell you his name now if you put a gun to her head. But she remembered that first cigarette. It went down hard.

She scrolled down the accident report.

The name of the driver: Jeffrey Halliwell.

The name of the passenger: Mike Levine.

"Huh," she said again.

Drano

Maybe it was the coffee.

There was none in the house, so he ventured out for a cup. A Starbucks around the corner. Around every corner now in New York. Across the street from one another.

It was stronger than he seemed to remember coffee ever tasting. A lot less watered down, or perhaps he'd been making it too weak, the beans too old, ground too fine.

Perhaps there was a reason people shelled out two bucks for a cup of the stuff.

But he could write. At least. It was as if some dam had been bombed, some clog removed. Someone had poured liquid Drano onto his brain, allowing it to run smoothly now.

The coffee.

Maybe it was because he could finally push Dina aside and concentrate. On the words. Their relationship to one another. How one sentence could so complement another, yet clash with the one that followed. A race war of sentiments and similes.

Clearheadedness.

He needed to believe that she was sincere in her apology. He wanted to think that she'd make no further appearances in his life.

That Dina was gone.

As heartbreaking as that felt.

Dina

The violation was intoxicating.

Peter was inside her, moving slowly at first, then abruptly picking up speed, despite her protests to slow back down. Those endless legs wrapped around his, her hands gripping the back of his neck, her mouth tracing small kisses around his nipples and chest.

Husband and wife.

Bliss reduced to boredom.

Dina watched them from the darkness of their bedroom closet, through the slightest open crack of the door. She'd been there for hours, sneaking in when they were out. Violating their space in any way she could. Leaving her own scent to remind Peter who really rocked his world.

She wished watching them turned her on so she could have joined in their pleasure, at least abstractly. But there was something routine and soft about their passion. Something inherently bland about the way they went about their business. It was soft-core, all the naughty bits and close-ups removed.

Maybe this was making love.

It certainly wasn't fucking.

After they'd fallen asleep, Dina quietly pushed the closet door open and crawled on all fours from her hiding space. In one hand she gripped Peter's notebook, the one from which *Angel* was born.

Fearlessly, perhaps a little foolishly, Dina moved over to Julianna's side of the bed, watching her sleep, smelling Peter on her breath. She remembered the smell well. And as if answering her own dare, she leaned forward and kissed her softly on the lips.

"I love you," Julianna whispered in her sleep.

Dina smiled, watching as the woman turned and spooned her husband.

Then, standing, Dina walked over to Peter's side of the bed. Could she satisfy him without ever waking the wife? she wondered. Or would waking Julianna be the best part?

She let that notion linger for a moment, her eyes unexpectedly drawn away from the main attraction. She focused now on Julianna's silver charm bracelet, aglow in the blue of the clock light, resting as it always did, always would, on Peter's nightstand.

Lifting it from the small circle of dust that seemed to protect it, Dina clasped the bracelet around her left wrist.

"How pretty," she whispered.

Tiptoeing down the hallway, she found the door to Kimberly's bedroom just cracked open. The little girl was sound asleep when Dina entered the room and approached her bed. Sitting softly on one edge, Dina leaned forward and, with her right hand, so as not to make any noise with her new trinket, she stroked Kimberly's hair.

Dina wished she had some childhood memory of her mother stroking her hair. Of anyone showing her any love, or compassion, or even attention.

She wished she could remember what it was like to feel young.

Or wanted.

Her final stop was Peter's office.

There she found Groucho fast asleep in front of the desk. The tip of the dog's tail wagged tentatively when he awoke and spotted the intruder. Then he rolled over on his back, paws up, as if begging for attention.

"Some guard dog you are," she said, bending at the knee, rubbing the dog's belly.

Then, taking a seat at Peter's desk, she sat back, far back in his chair, feeling so at home. As if she could live in this room, die in this room. She felt she certainly had been born here.

She closed her eyes for a moment and pictured her time with him in the room in Madison. How she wanted more. How she wished she had taken more right then, on the spot. He would have given in. He would have given her anything she wanted.

But she thought at the time that less was more. A hint of what was to come. A tease.

Shaking her head, thinking this was taking so much longer than she anticipated, she sat forward, placing his notebook square on the desk. Then snatching a Post-it note from a dispenser hiding behind Peter's stapler, Dina scribbled a short note.

Thanks for sharing, it read.

Kodak Moment

"Honey, have you seen my charm bracelet?"

Dressed for work in another in a long line of power suits, one that seemed particularly sexy in Peter's mind, Julianna rushed up to her husband as he leaned back against the kitchen counter. She took the coffee cup from his hands and had a sip.

"I can't find it anywhere," she said.

"When do you remember seeing it last?"

"I'm sure I took it off before we went to bed. Put it on the night table like usual."

He grinned. "Maybe we knocked it off last night."

"That was the first place I looked," she said, "under the bed." She motioned toward the paper cup in his hands, the all-too-familiar logo. "We out of coffee?"

He shook his head. "Just tastes better than what I can make. Fuel for the typing frenzy."

"A new bad habit?"

"I needed one," he said.

"Then buy me a latte tomorrow morning," she said, "and a low-fat banana muffin. I could use another bad habit as well."

"Yes, ma'am," he said.

She took the cup again, another sip.

"Definitely stronger," she said.

"Ready?"

Julianna looked at their daughter, dressed and ready for school. Then, sighing loudly, she turned back to Peter.

"The bracelet," he said. "I know. Don't worry; I'll find it."

On the way down the hall to his office, Peter stopped to adjust a framed photograph taken at the book party his publisher threw to celebrate the arrival of *Angel* in stores. It was just a popular pizza joint over on Second Avenue, with twenty or so friends. But it was one of the happiest days of his life.

Staring at the image, at the way Julianna looked at him in the photograph. So proud, so . . . It was the way you'd want the love of your life to look at you, always. She wore a little black party dress that night, her hair down, everything about her long and beautiful. The charm bracelet glinting off her wrist, the only accessory. No other accessories needed.

Mike was off to one side, smiling for the camera. His assistant, Sandra, stood beside *Angel*'s editor and that editor's boss, who owned the publishing house. The room seemed crowded, so many faces, so many—

That was when he noticed her.

In the background, the same eyes, same hair, same . . . He pulled the photo from the wall to get a better look.

Angling it to soften the reflection of the light,

squinting, wondering how he could have not noticed her way back then, he began to laugh at his own jumpiness.

Not Dina, not even close.

Just a poster-size reproduction of the *Angel* cover, hung on a wall behind them. The eyes so lifelike and real, it seemed as if Dina were part of the crowd.

As if she were real way back then.

Still amused, Peter opened the door to his office and spotted it immediately.

He could feel the color drain from his face, a light-headedness powered by the rush of caffeine. Placing the coffee cup down on his desktop, he picked up his old notebook, and read Dina's message once, then again, and again, crumpling it finally into a tight ball, tossing it angrily to the floor.

He began pacing the room, notebook in hand, his color returning with a vengeance. Flipping through the pages, the ideas he'd jotted down what seemed like so long ago, a lifetime ago. A slip of paper fluttering free like a trapped moth, dying in midflight, falling to the floor.

He remembered the writing, the note, the warning, Halliwell ripping out the page, handing him what he thought he needed. All in the name of research.

Raoul.

And the phone number that started it all.

Slapping open his cellular, Peter dialed.

"Speak," came the grizzled voice at the other end of the line.

"It's Peter Robertson."

A hair of silence, then: "Yo, man. How's it hanging? You doin' some more of that . . . reeesearch?"

"Something like that," Peter said. "Got a minute to spare?"

"Yeah," Raoul responded. "I think I can squeeze you in."

Perpetual States

One of the seven deadly sins answered the door.

Lust incarnated into a gorgeous barefoot Hispanic girl wearing only the skimpiest of bras and skintight velour shorts. Her face was a sculpture of pouty innocence, with freckles still flashing her cheeks, her body everything but, dark and just fleshy enough in all the right places.

"I'm here to see Raoul," Peter said, knowing he was wrong, but hating the girl nonetheless, blaming her for the Halliwells of the world, blaming her for the men who couldn't control their urges. Blaming her for desires she could never control.

The door opened wider, revealing Raoul standing just behind her, the owner, the master. The man forced a big smile, holding out one oversize hand.

Shaking it, looking into the once ferocious man's eyes, only one thought came now to Peter's mind.

You don't look well.

More elaborate than before, or perhaps the people who designed the toys were just getting smarter. Everything smaller, tighter, newer, a sleeker design.

Even the girl.

"Juicy, get us some beer," Raoul barked.

He gave her a slap on the ass, upon which the word JUICY was written in large white letters. She made a face, but obeyed his orders.

"That really her name, Juicy?" Peter asked once she was out of earshot.

"No." Raoul laughed. "It's just the perpetual state of her pussy. Wanna see what I mean?"

"No," Peter said. "But thanks for offering."

"Same ol' Peter—you can look, but no touching allowed."

"Some things never change."

"They changed for our friend Halliwell," Raoul said, *tsk*ing. "What a shame."

"That must have put a dent in your profits."

"Mine *and* Juicy's. Jeffrey was one of her regular customers."

That didn't surprise Peter. "Like with Lucinda?" he asked.

The mention of her name brought a flash of anger to Raoul's eyes. "Don't you mean Angel?"

"No," Peter said, holding his ground, not finding the man nearly as threatening as he once did. Time changed perception. Time softened muscle. Time corroded the soul. Time made you careless. "I meant Lucinda."

"Lucinda is history," Raoul said. "I don't live in the past."

How about the future? Peter thought, asking, "Have the cops been by?"

"No." A sudden twitch in Raoul's neck, jolting his head ever so slightly to the right. "Why?"

"Seems my name was on Halliwell's Palm Pilot," Peter explained. "Just wondering if yours was as well."

"The dude liked to party. That didn't mean he was whacked."

Peter nodded again, just barely this time.

"So, what do you need?" Raoul asked.

"A gun."

Raoul laughed as Juicy returned with two beers, handing one to each man.

"Thank you," Peter said.

"Is there anything else I could get you?" she asked, just like Lucinda, only better.

"You can get yourself lost," Raoul answered for Peter. "You're not Mr. Robertson's type."

"Yes, I am," Juicy replied, smiling at the novelist, backing away, but holding on to Peter's look.

"You're fuckin' with me, right?" Raoul asked.

After a long pause, during which Peter wondered how a girl her age could so sneak into the deep recesses of his mind to read desires he couldn't begin to fathom, he turned to face Raoul, shaking his head boldly.

"How 'bout this instead," Raoul offered. "I'll lend you Juicy for an hour; she'll fix whatever's wrong, and then some. Make you forget why you ever wanted a gun in the first place." He laughed. "Be kinda eye-opening to read your take on the effect a little spic girl can have on a straitlaced WASP."

Peter stared him down, holding his look until it was Raoul who turned away.

"Then again . . ." Raoul said.

Standing reluctantly, he reached up to the top of a bookcase, retrieving an automatic pistol. He checked it, removed the clip, then handed the pistol to Peter.

"A Beretta Cheetah .380," Raoul explained, displaying the pistol in one hand, the clip in the other. "Thirteen-shot clip."

Peter didn't blink. "How much?" he asked.

"I paid six hundred. You can have it for that."

Peter opened his wallet and handed over the cash. Shaking his head in complete dismay, Raoul handed over the Beretta.

"Motherfucking Peter Gunn," he muttered.

Reasonable

Another door.

Another sin.

She answered wearing that same tank top, or one just like it, no jeans this time, just panties. She shot him a cursory glance, disgusted. As if she had any goddamn right to be disgusted with him. Turning back into her apartment, she let the door swing open. There was a bounce to her step as she walked to the sofa. A lot sexier than her mood might have suggested.

"I'm ready if you are," she said, lying back, middle pillow, full slouch, her legs open. There was no mistaking the look on her face, or the pleasures left unspoken.

Peter tried to remain calm. He shut the door to her apartment, then walked over to the sofa, taking a seat on the edge of the coffee table across from her. Dina looked for a second as if she thought Peter might take her up on the offer. *About freakin' time.* But the tone in his voice shot that notion to hell.

"I'm going to tell you this once, Dina."

"What, Peter? What are you going to tell me?"

"Stay away from my family," he said. "Stay out of my life."

She sat forward so that they were face-to-face. She could have kissed him quickly, if she had wanted to, but instead offered up an indiscriminate shrug, as if she couldn't care less.

"And if I don't?" she replied.

"I'll kill you," Peter said without hesitation.

She matched his lack of emotion beat for beat. "You couldn't. You—"

He slapped her hard across the face before she could say another word. She fell back onto the sofa, staring at him with wide, frightened eyes. The look of an injured animal, or a child. As if she were the one betrayed.

Straddling her violently, holding her by the throat, Peter pulled the gun from the pocket of his coat and jammed it under her chin. She flinched, clenching her eyes shut.

"Try me," he said, his voice so distant and cold even he didn't recognize it.

For once, Dina was silent.

These were not the actions of a reasonable man.

How could he be doing this to her? What had happened? What had gotten into him? He tried to think of no one other than Julianna and Kimberly. He was here for their safety. For the safety of his family. The sanctity of his family, his marriage. He was here.

Pulling the gun back, putting it away and standing, Peter headed toward the door. He just wanted out. But hearing the rage build behind him, the footsteps, the guttural scream, he spun around just in time to catch her fists before they could pound onto his back.

Slamming her up against a wall so hard books fell off an adjacent shelf. Holding her still. Their breathing jagged and short. But in sync.

Until he noticed the bracelet.

Julianna's charm bracelet on Dina's wrist. Ripping it off in a fit of rage, all compassion gone. Wanting just to snuff her life out right then and there and get it over with. Peter grabbed her face with such force her could feel her jawbone begin to snap. His words were lethal now and measured.

"As far as I'm concerned, you don't exist," he told her. "You never have. Killing you would mean nothing to me."

Stepping back, letting go with a push against a wall that could take no more. Dina fell to the floor, pulling herself into a tight fetal ball.

She was sobbing by the time Peter slammed the door shut on her existence.

PART FOUR

Angel

The first night alone was the hardest.

It felt like abandonment, but hadn't she run away? Hadn't she escaped? Hadn't she driven him to despise her so? Why else would he do those . . . things?

Her first night alone in . . . ?

A soft, whimpering cry from some other part of the room. She pulled the sheets and blanket over her head, pulling herself tight into a ball. A familiar position, for all the wrong reasons.

Fuck! She couldn't remember how long it had been.

If not by his side, or with a regular, then lying beneath whatever john was willing to pay for a girl to spend the night. And that rarely meant sleep. It got to the point that she dreaded the overnight calls and the haze of drugs and booze that usually went with them. It was the only way Angel could make it through.

The bed was comfortable enough, the blanket a little threadbare, the sheets even more so. They smelled of generic fabric softener, the room of cleaning products and air fresheners. But she convinced herself this was only a pit stop. The manhole cover had been pried open, and this was a step up the ladder. She could see the daylight overhead. The cars passing. Pedestrians. Baby carriages and dogs being walked.

If only the girl on the other side of the room would stop crying. Angel wanted to scream, but she had been on the other side of such ranting. Especially at the end. Begging for a break. Telling him how badly it hurt. It only made him madder.

She wondered if he thought her dead now. Or just gone. Or if he even cared.

Had another girl already taken her place?

The women who ran the shelter had been nice so far. Food, some less obvious clothing, counseling, a TV, games, books— just like home. Even classes that might help her get a job.

She'd had a job. She'd been an entrepreneur at thirteen.

Tears came to her eyes—she told herself that, goddammit, she wouldn't cry—as she thought back to her home in the West Village, her mom, that life, the secrets that so excited her then. She'd made the decision never to return, never to see her mother again. At one point it seemed a small price to pay. So deluded, so drugged.

She thought of Richard.

And all the things he'd given her, taught her.

All the things he'd taken.

He'd taken her to Saint Barts once.

Right after she'd left home for good.

Paid ten thousand dollars for the pleasure of her company. Ten thousand dollars.

She broke it down once. That came to less than four hundred seventeen dollars per sexual act. A bargain for Richard, actually, compared to what he usually paid back then.

She wondered now if he ever realized she'd have gone for free.

Blank Canvas Waiting

It was as if the rage had turned to inspiration.

An all-nighter, or perhaps it was more than just one night. Many nights. Countless nights. Locking himself in, no respite for the wicked. It was the pressure of the deadline. The promise to his daughter. Not breaking that promise.

Maybe it was the hope that life would once again return to normal.

To hand in the pages. Forget about them for a while. A vacation, or just a break. To rest. To sleep. To figure out what would come next. What might. What could. The next book. A comedy. Or at least something lighter. Definitely lighter in tone, in subject matter.

"No Angels," he said out loud as he held down the CONTROL button on his computer keyboard with the thumb of his left hand; then with the index finger of his right he pressed P.

It was over.

The printer spit out pages.

Peter sat hypnotized before his monitor, blank now,

another canvas waiting. A funeral in motion, from the sound of the machine. The dirge. A procession. The *suck-whir-spit, suck-whir-spit.* The fan cooling it all down. Preventing the overheat. We all needed fans installed.

He heard the knock, but didn't turn, didn't respond.

"Peter?" Her voice muffled though the closed door.

After a beat he forced himself to smile, to put on a good face, to release the characters once and for all and go back. Then he stood and answered the door.

Julianna was half-asleep. "It was locked," she said.

"Must have hit the button by accident," he explained, pushing the grin now so that she'd notice.

"What are you doing in here?" she asked, yawning. "You never came to bed." Noticing. "Is something wrong?"

He swung the door open wide, and her eyes were drawn immediately to the sound of the printer.

"I'm done."

It felt strange for Peter to say those words.

As Julianna stared at the freshly minted pages, Peter pulled her charm bracelet from his pants pocket and held it in her line of sight.

"I even found this," he said.

Her eyes flooded with tears of recognition and relief.

"Thank you," she whispered, throwing her arms around her husband's neck.

"You're welcome," he said, never wanting to let her go.

Weight of the Word

He stood watching her for a few moments through the double glass doors, his eyes blurring the gold leaf of the word *Literary*.

She sat before her computer, typing, raising her left hand time and again to cup the side of her face with her fingertips. Then raising that hand to her forehead, scratching a nail lightly down the bridge of her nose, then returning it to the keyboard.

Her name meant "helper of humanity." Her boss's "who is like God." He wondered how much Sandra knew about the habits that boss shared with Jeffrey Halliwell, "God's peace."

And would it have made any difference to her?

He opened the door and stepped inside the office.

"Hey, Peter," she said, looking up, using her left hand now to push the flowing strands of blond behind one ear.

He needed to believe it would make all the difference in the world.

"Hi, Sandra," he said, then motioned with his chin toward Mike's office. "He in?"

"He's actually over at Random House closing a deal."

Nodding thoughtfully, Peter pulled the boxed manuscript from his messenger bag, its leather now worn, creased, cracked. The veneer showing its age, stress, that perhaps it carried a little too much weight.

Sandra stood, her face awash in surprise. "Oh, my God! Is that it?"

Nodding, Peter asked, "May I put it on his desk?"

"Go right ahead," she said. "He'll be thrilled."

Peter leaned over his agent's desk, the manuscript in front of him, his hands pressing flat on either side, knuckles white from the pressure, the pain, the release.

Something had to give, he thought. The desk or bones in his hands. Wanting it to be both, one final push down into hell, falling with the trace history of signatures like death warrants and foreclosures. To burn and relieve the guilt.

Stepping back suddenly, an explosion of air in his lungs. *Not here*, he thought. *Not here*. He snatched a Sharpie from his bag and scribbled a note for Mike on the box.

Be careful what you wish for, he wrote.

The End of the Ride

He stepped into the elevator car, pressing the already
lit L for lobby. Pressing back past the other three passengers, taking position against the mirrored rear wall
of the empty car, he looked out across the lobby at another bank of elevator doors. The car directly across the
way landed with a ding. Its doors opened just as the
doors to the car Peter was riding in began to shut.

And there she was.

Dressed in black, as always, but now with a scarf
around her neck, and dark glasses. Her hair hanging
long and loose, as if covering a sin. She seemed more
angry than battered.

Dina.

Stepping from the other car, glaring at him, as if
she'd been watching, following, timing it all out.

Peter lunged forward as she stepped toward Mike's
office, but it was too late. The doors shut tightly on his
escape, and the car started moving.

With the three other riders backing away, he furiously pressed the buttons for the next few floors below.

When the elevator finally stopped on fifteen, Peter

pushed through the just-opening door. He headed for the stairs.

Taking them three at a time, not thinking about the breath he needed, instead just about what she might do, why she might do it. It made no sense to follow him here, but then, none of this made sense to him. Dina made no sense.

He pushed through the fire door, rushing toward Mike's office, pulling on one of the two glass doors.

Stopping in place.

Deserted.

Even Sandra, gone.

Entering slowly, Peter looked around for some sign of life. Passing her desk, peering into Mike's office.

The boxed manuscript was as he'd left it, sitting still atop the desk.

"Forget something?"

Turning quickly, his fist clenched, he came face-to-face with Sandra, who stood just behind him.

Startled, she gasped.

"Oh," he said. "I'm sorry. No . . . I, ah . . . thought I saw a friend coming into the office, and I had already pressed the button for the lobby."

Smiling warmly now, in that assistantly way, she said, "Nope, not here. No one's been in except you. Quiet day. Fridays usually are."

Shaking his head at the visions clouding it, hoping perhaps to shake them free, Peter entered another elevator car. This one packed. The doors slid shut; the ride began.

Glancing up, watching the floor numbers light up,

then die, he spotted the round security mirror. Focusing in on it. Something catching his attention.

Staring right back at him.

Glaring through him.

Dina.

He looked down toward the floor as the breath caught in his chest. Slipping a hand into his messenger bag, he found his one piece of security, grabbing the grip of his pistol. Holding it securely, as if for dear life.

Not turning back, not daring to look, he waited for the inevitable ding that would signal the end of the ride.

Pillars of Stone

Peter pressed forward through the just-opening door, moving with a purpose, his legs tight, his body stiff, as if bracing for the attack, the bite of the dog, to die.

The sea of faces made him dizzy. The salmon-colored marble splashes of wall and tile. Scenes from a movie played in his head, where he could scale those walls, turn, fall, firing weapons from both hands. Dina the enemy, her face multiplying, her face on everybody, every man, woman, child. Converging on him now, coming toward him.

His chest clenching, his left arm numb, not a shortness of breath, but no breath at all. He pushed up against the first of those marble columns, feeling his way around it, hiding from the Dinas exiting the elevator car.

He held on to the pistol as best he could.

Waiting.

Forcing the breath into his lungs and back again.

Willing the throb in his temples under some sort of control.

Banging his left arm back against the pillar of stone,

beating the blood into submission, hurting it until the feeling returned.

Waiting.

For Dina.

But Dina.

Never came.

Life As He Knew It

She wasn't crying this time.

Waiting for him on the steps as he ran, as if to her rescue.

"You forgot about me again, Daddy," she called as he approached. "I hope you don't forget you're coming to class next week. Show-and-tell, remember?"

Sweeping her up into his arms. "Yes, pumpkin, of course. I could never forget about you."

"It's okay this time," Kimberly said, "Some nice lady kept me company."

"What lady?" Peter asked, a little confused now, lowering his daughter back to the ground, squatting down so that they were eye-to-eye.

"She was really pretty," Kimberly said. "She had black hair. She even knew my name."

He could feel the panic rising. "What'd she say to you?"

"That she was my daddy's biggest fan."

Straightening up, standing, Peter looked around, turning a three-sixty, feeling the street turn against him, trying to spot her, to see her. He clenched and unclenched his left hand over and again, wanting to feel. Wanting to know how she beat him down here. How she knew where Kimberly went to school.

She was pulling at his sleeve.

"Can we go home now, Daddy?"

"Sure, pumpkin," he said, taking her hand. Squeezing her hand. "Let's go."

"The lady said there was going to be a surprise for us there."

"At home?"

"Uh-huh."

Life as he knew it flashed before his eyes, a bad music video of everything he had taken for granted, crashed and cracked and set on fire like the lead guitarist's Stratocaster. The end credits were rolling. Too fast. He couldn't read them. Couldn't see who was to blame.

With breath exploding from his lungs, he turned and swept his daughter up into his arms.

He ran home.

Knowing the only name on those credits was his.

Groucho

Groucho was a mutt.

Peter had adopted the abused and abandoned dog from an animal shelter the day before Groucho was scheduled to be put to sleep. A mostly yellow Lab/shepherd mix, he was about a year and a half old at the time, maybe a little less, full-grown but with puppy enthusiasm, barely trained, his tail half-missing from what mishap Peter could only imagine. He'd been passed over so many times. "People want puppies," the woman at the shelter explained. "Or purebloods." Groucho wasn't close to either. And with his nose an off-color shade of pink, a tuft of black fur just under that nose, and dark, bushy patches of hair over his big brown eyes, he was sort of weird-looking. But something in those eyes begged Peter to give him a second chance at life.

That was nine years back.

Peter rushed into his apartment.

"Groucho!" he called out, moving at such a clip that

he banged into Kimberly's small desk in the living room, catching himself and stumbling back to his feet before hitting the ground.

Kimberly followed behind him cautiously, shooting her dad a strange look.

"What's wrong, Daddy?"

"Nothing, pumpkin," he said. "Everything is fine."

Rushing down the hallway, his daughter right behind him, Peter looked first into his bedroom, then hers, the bathroom . . . nothing.

"What are you looking for?" she asked.

He raised a finger to his lips, shushing her, just as a noise caught his attention.

"You hear that?" he said, thinking he heard a whimper or a whine.

Listening intently, then nodding, Kimberly pointed at his office door.

"In there, Daddy," she said excitedly, as if into playing this particular game.

With his right hand buried deep in his messenger bag, Peter slowly turned the door handle to his office. He had the door open only a crack when Groucho lunged through the doorway, jumping on Peter, knocking him to the floor, licking his face.

He could hear his daughter laughing hysterically as he scratched the dog behind the ears and worked his way up to a sitting position.

That was when he smelled the smoke.

Turning, glancing through the now-open doorway, Peter stared in stunned disbelief, eyeing a smoldering mass atop his desk.

Pulling himself to his knees, hoping his daughter

didn't notice, hoping he could clean off the burn, disguise the smell, he heard the familiar jangle of keys as the door to his apartment opened, and Julianna announced: "Guess who took the afternoon off?"

Promise

"Mommy!" Kimberly screamed in delight.

Peter turned to see Julianna walking though their living room toward him. It was a vision he had trouble pulling himself from. But turning back toward his office, the fright, the sight. He could never explain it—that Dina had been in their home.

"What are you doing on the floor?" she asked.

He attempted an excuse, but the words never came. Instead he noticed her smile. She looked more relaxed than he could remember her in a very long while.

Giggling loudly, their daughter answered for him: "Groucho knocked Daddy over."

"How'd that happen?"

"He was in my office," Peter said, pulling himself to his feet. "Must have pushed the door shut. Got himself trapped."

"In that spooky place?" Julianna said.

"Mommy just called your office spooky," Kimberly said. More giggles.

"Mommy's right," Peter said, catching his wife just as she hit the office doorway, holding her shoulders, turning her, kissing her, trying to distract her, trying to keep her back to the room.

The kiss lingered long past what he would have expected. "Mommy's always right," she said, holding his look for a beat. Then: "Let me get out of my lawyer suit so we can play."

"Yea," Kimberly cried out, hearing one of her favorite words.

Smiling, Peter watched his wife walk toward the bedroom, with Kimberly trailing after her, skipping for joy; then he stepped into the office to clean up Dina's mess.

It was the first edition of *Angel* he signed for her back in Madison. Charred, but still recognizable, Peter's stiletto stabbed into the cover of the book, right between the girl's eyes.

Staring at the image Dina had created, Angel, an eternity in hell after someone had taken her life. Or perhaps she'd taken her own after all. Decided that death was the only way to escape her past. And everything that came after her break, from the moment she entered the shelter onward, was just an illusion, some sickeningly sweet fantasy rubbish that she could start over; she could survive.

Was it an extra hundred pages of nonsense? Was the new book more of the same?

Just as Peter angrily shoved the book into the crawl space behind the bookcase, Julianna, now dressed in jeans and a T-shirt, popped her head into his office.

"How's it feel?" she asked.

He couldn't look at her at first, the confusion and guilt a blinding combo. "How's what feel?"

"Now that it's over . . . the book?"

Standing, nodding, he forced a small laugh.

"Still not used . . . to . . . it . . ." he said, the words trailing off.

"What?"

"Nothing," he said, trying to calm the rage, hoping she wouldn't follow his line of sight, notice his stare. To avoid it, he looked around, at anything but the shredded *Angel* T-shirt hung on the coat hook, where Dina herself once hung, on the inside of his office door.

"Just . . . um . . . good, I guess," he blurted out. "I mean . . . you know, finishing a book is always a little strange for me. Like ending a friendship."

"More like an affair this time," Julianna said, laughing.

"How so?"

"Oh, c'mon. Tell me you haven't always had a crush on Angel. That's why you couldn't let her go."

"She's not real," Peter argued.

"That doesn't mean you want her any less," she said playfully. "But that's okay. You can have crushes on all the fictional characters you want. As long as you save the real thing for me."

Julianna turned to leave but shot him back a sexy grin laced with adoration as she exited his office.

She never even noticed the T-shirt.

Disconnected (Again)

The front left side of the building.

Two windows. No curtains. No blinds. No shades.

He hadn't noticed when he was inside, but now, staring up from across the street . . . The immodesty. A stereo slide show into her life. A View-Master.

Apparently Dina had nothing to hide.

How long had he been standing there? It had been daylight when he left his apartment. And now lights were coming on inside apartment windows. Not hers. Not yet.

Holding hard on to the side of his messenger bag, feeling the shape of the gun through the leather, Peter looked up and down the street for a pay phone, but spotted none. When had all the pay phones disappeared? And anonymity with them?

Slapping open his cellular, he punched in her number from memory now, as if he'd called it a thousand times in his head. Though this was never the call he imagined. In the fantasy version he said simply, *I need to see you now.* But fantasies were best if they remained just that. Even dreams were oftentimes best left in your head. He understood that now.

At the end of the ring, the sound of the connection, Peter jumped right down her throat.

"What the fuck do you think you're doing?" he screamed.

The answer took him by surprise.

"The number you have dialed has been disconnected or is no longer in service. Please hang up and try your call again."

Glaring upward, wanting to catch her spying on him, feeling her eyes burn, her disdain, hearing her snickers. Her reason for not turning the lights on yet. He dialed her number again, listening this time, the results identical.

He slapped shut the phone, wanting just to fling it to the ground, or across the street, wanting to hurl it through her goddamn window five stories up.

But instead he took a deep breath, then another. And, pocketing the cellular, he crossed the street and entered building number 571, his right hand slipping into his bag as the door swung shut behind him.

This would end now.

A Ghost Is Born

He knocked.

Nothing, not a sound.

"Open the fucking door, Dina. I know you're in there."

He banged louder this time, his hand clenched into a fist.

Nothing. Except the echo of his rage and frustration off plaster walls and a century's worth of paint.

She wasn't doing this, breaking into his life, then refusing him entrance into hers.

Shaking his head, mouthing words he so wanted to say to her, picturing the fear in her eyes as she realized she'd pushed him too far, Peter glanced down to the far end of the hallway, listening for any signs of life.

Hearing none, he rammed his shoulder hard into the door, pushing his way into her apartment.

He didn't know what happened.

He couldn't explain it.

Instead he just stood, stunned and confused.

Flipping on the light, a bare bulb in an overhead, he looked around her apartment, empty now, categorically stale. No furniture, no belongings. No sign of life or death. No sign of Dina.

Just empty rooms with naked walls and floors.

Lonely promise.

It looked as if no one had lived there for years.

Feeling a shortness of breath, a tightening that made it hurt to breathe, Peter moved quickly down the hallway, pushing into her bedroom, flipping on the light, finding nothing but a plain empty box, no shelves, no hidden space, no stained-glass window of the Virgin Mary blessing every proceeding.

Never how he'd have imagined it.

Into her bathroom, empty except for the water stains, the mildew, the slight stench.

Stopping at the sink, holding on to the sides, trying to slow his descent, Peter turned the cold water faucet on. It farted and choked, but then the water came. Filling his cupped hands, he splashed some onto his face over and again a few times, standing up finally, catching his reflection in the mirror.

Pale, shaking, as if he'd seen a ghost.

Or lost one.

Peter, Raoul, and Dina

"You on something, man?"

Raoul looked him up and down, a creased forehead mixed with equal parts disdain and concern. He never allowed junkies to bring their problems home to the source, and he certainly wasn't about to start now. And though he'd never given Peter Robertson so much as a snort or a drag, this was motherfucking strung-out time if ever he saw it.

"No, I ah . . ."

"Bullshit!"

"I'm not on anything," Peter said. "I swear." He shot a look back over his shoulder that made Raoul poke his head farther out the door.

"Whatcha looking for then?" Raoul asked.

"Nothing," Peter said. "Nothing. I just . . ." He shook his head and tried to focus. *You can do this, you can do this, you can do this,* he said over and over to himself, thinking of Julianna, thinking of Kimberly, thinking even of Groucho.

Then calmly, forced and desperate, the fright, the paranoia inching away, he added, "Can I come in?"

Raoul held his gaze for a beat, then slid the door open just wide enough for him to pass.

"Just remember where you are," Raoul said.

"You alone?" Peter asked.

"Why do you need to know that?"

"I just . . . I don't want anyone else to hear what I have to say."

"Why not? You suddenly got something to hide?"

"I need advice."

Raoul laughed. "Advice?"

"Yes."

"What the fuck, from me?"

"There's this . . . girl."

"And what, you think I understand 'em better than anyone else? That I've got some secret insight into what makes them do the shit they do?"

"She broke into my house."

"You don't say."

"Twice now," Peter explained, thinking. "No, three times. Three times she was there. What would you do?"

"It wouldn't be happening to me," Raoul said jokingly, but when Peter didn't respond, not even a smile: "You really asking me?"

"I don't know how to handle this."

"But you want it taken care of?"

"I want it over," Peter said.

"Okay, then," Raoul said, a beat to reflect. "Next time, I'd be sitting on my La-Z-Boy, just waiting for that bitch with a big-ass grin on my face, a blunt in one hand, and that motherfucking Beretta in the other." He took aim at his own door with his fingers, like a gun. "Boom," he added calmly. "You've bought it, man. Use it."

Watching Peter walk down the street, Raoul knew it was the last time he'd let the novelist into his home. Peter had entered the twilight zone, and Raoul had enough crazies in his life as it was.

A sudden chill struck him odd and hard. It was colder than it should have been for this time of the year, and Raoul hated the cold. Juicy would need to warm him up when she got home. But she was good at that. Feeling the goose bumps slither down his spine and away, he checked his watch to calculate how long before she returned, then headed back into his apartment.

Dina waited a few beats after the door had been slammed shut to step from the shadows. Pulling a pair of handcuffs from her purse—the handcuffs from Peter's desk—she held them behind her back, stepped over to Raoul's door, and rang the bell.

Won't he be surprised to see me again? she thought.

The Best Offense

He needed to make a decision.

He had to act defensively.

It wasn't a case where he could wait for it to be too late. It wasn't something he might be able to fix after the fact. Who knew what Dina might do? How she might behave?

From his vantage point on the right cushion of their old dark green sofa, Peter stared down lovingly at his daughter, who played with her toys on the floor. If anything happened to her, how could he ever forgive himself? How could he ever live?

"Hey, you."

He looked over to see Julianna standing in the entrance to the kitchen. She was wiping her hands with a kitchen towel, the bracelet jangling on her wrist, as it always did, as it always should.

"You're supposed to be happy," she said. "It's over."

If only that were true, he thought, nodding nonetheless, then standing, going to her, following her back into the kitchen, watching as she reached for her coat.

"Where're you going?" he asked.

"I'm making something special for dinner tonight, and we need a good bottle of wine to go with it," she said, then added with a smile, "Two good bottles of wine. We have something to celebrate."

"Let me go," he said, not wanting her to leave, not wanting her out there. Not tonight.

"You sure?"

"I'm sure," he said, kissing her softly on the lips good-bye.

Juicy

Juicy didn't hate Raoul.

Not the way those looking in might have believed.

She actually liked the guy. He treated her well. Made her laugh. Bought her nice clothes. Took her to fancy restaurants. He even flew her to Puerto Rico once. A working vacation was what he called it, but still, she had fun. Fucking strangers in Puerto Rico was a hell of a lot better than doing it in a Midtown hotel.

She got her keys out, as she always did, crossing Avenue D. Holding them tightly in her right hand, a weapon if need be. Not that anyone would mess with her. Raoul carried enough weight and respect to offer a safe haven, even on suspect boulevards.

There were two dead bolts and a latch that caught itself no matter what. Slipping her key into the first lock, she turned counterclockwise, but nothing gave, as if the lock had never been locked to begin with. She barely noticed, and might not have, had the second dead bolt also not been locked.

"Raoul, you're going senile," she muttered, shaking her head, adding a couple of curses in her native tongue.

At least the latch had caught.

Juicy disappeared into the apartment. The clicks of the two dead bolts locking were like snap-tos on the otherwise empty street. No sirens, no babies crying from fourth-floor windows, no dogs barking, no TV blaring. Even the traffic, the tourists daring for a parking space a few blocks east of their trendy eateries, was missing in action.

The world had become as quiet as Peter's blank page.

Until Juicy's scream.

Segregation

The aisles so long, the shelves so tall. The darkened glass of the cork-topped bottles for as far as the eye could see. Broken down into countries, like a geography lesson. The whites, of course, segregated from the reds. The blushes in a ghetto all their own.

He stood before Australia. Julianna liked Australian wines. He remembered that well. But he couldn't pick up a bottle, not a shiraz, not a merlot, not until his hands stopped shaking. And it seemed as if they'd been shaking for a very long while.

Looking up and down the aisle, wondering.

Could she find him in a place like this?

Could she be watching him now?

Or would she be on her way back to his apartment, knowing his wife and daughter were alone?

His cellular rang as he stepped from the package store.

"Hello," he said.

"I'm tired of the games, Peter."

"So am I," he replied, not needing to hear anymore.

He snapped the phone shut and headed not in the direction of home, but toward the closest subway station, where he'd ride the number six train to Fifty-ninth Street, the Mike Levine stop.

Peter always rode the local.

Never the express.

Rossi

Raoul sat in a puddle of his own blood on a rug at the foot of his king-size bed. The rug, Persian and pricey, was purple now, soaked, its hieroglyphics of leaves and flowers forever destroyed by its owner's DNA.

His hands were handcuffed over his lollygagging head to the bed's wrought-iron footboard. He'd bled out from a single stab wound to the chest. Not a hit meant to kill instantly, but slowly.

Raoul had watched himself die.

But at least he hadn't been alone at the time.

Detective Rossi watched as the ME pulled open the victim's blood-soaked shirt. The wound was pinpoint and precise.

"Look familiar?" he asked.

"Jeffrey Halliwell?" she said.

As he nodded, Rossi walked back into the living room, where Juicy sat on the leather sectional, trembling and crying. She squatted down to one knee in front of the distraught girl so they were eye-to-eye.

"How long were you gone?" Rossi asked.

Juicy shrugged without looking at her. That was the extent of her answer.

"How long?" the detective asked again.

"Do I look like I wear a fucking watch?" Juicy answered, looking up this time, the fear in her face childlike despite her disposition.

Rossi held the girl's look until she gave in. Softening as best she could under the circumstances.

"I don't know," Juicy said, spitting out the words, tasting the disgust in her mouth, the bile of ancient memories. She didn't like the cops. The cops never did anything to protect her as a child. They never did anything to protect her mom. "Like . . ." She shrugged, trying to piece together time. Not easy when you were high. "Three hours maybe."

Rossi nodded. "Do you have any idea who might have wanted Mr. Santiago dead?"

Juicy bit down on her bottom lip and shook her head emphatically no. *He's dead,* she thought. *He's really gone.*

"Everyone loved Raoul," she said, wondering who'd take care of her now.

The squeak of a wheel in desperate need of oil caught their attention. They both shot looks back at the doorway to the bedroom, as Raoul's corpse was wheeled out on a gurney.

"Not everybody," Rossi said.

Blow Jobs and Balconies

"Fuck you!" he yelled, slamming shut the door in Peter's face.

Peter's hand caught it, pushing it open. Strength that surprised both men. Pressing his way into the apartment. Not bothering to ask. Just taking, as so much had been taken from him. He needed to talk. He needed to talk now.

"Help me, Mike," he said, trying to calm his voice, trying to make it unrelated to what he was feeling inside. Trying to forget about her—if only he *could* forget about her—for a moment.

"I told you I was tired of the games."

"I'm not the one who's playing the goddamn games," Peter cried.

"You sure you had the right building?" Mike asked.

Peter stood in front of the open sliding glass door that led out to the balcony. He stared at the skyline and thought of Christmas, stockings, gifts under the tree. What would a Christmas be without them?

"Yeah," he said finally. "It was Dina's apartment. The same apartment. No question."

"You told me she was crazy, but . . ."

"But?" Peter asked.

"But nothing. She's fucking with your head, man."

"You can't just disappear—"

Mike cut him off without sense of shame. "Sure you can."

Peter let some of the air escape his lungs. It was as if it were trapped there, a prisoner, breathing easily a lost memory. He remembered his bag with the two wine bottles. Turning, wondering where he'd left it. He couldn't go home without it.

"I was so sure I saw her go into your office today," Peter said, spotting the bag on Mike's coffee table. He needed to get home.

That comment caught Mike's attention. "When?"

"Right after I dropped off the manuscript."

Mike shook his head. "You've got to be kidding me."

"Why?"

"I'll show you."

Mike stepped to his kitchen, returning a second later with Peter's boxed manuscript. He handed him the box.

"That would explain this?"

Peter looked at him for a beat, then opened it. The cover page was as it should be.

The rest was not.

Eyeing the dedication page. The words *For Julianna and Kimberly, every word, always, for you* angrily crossed out in bloodred marker. He could sense the violence, the power, the resentment of the strokes. Flipping through, the rest blank, except for the page numbers and title at the top of every page.

Leaning over the coffee table, Mike pulled one of the bottles of wine from the paper bag. "I thought it was your way of telling me to piss off."

"I'd be more direct," Peter promised.

"I would hope so."

Standing, the weight of his sin crushing, Peter stepped out onto the deck for air. Mike was right behind him, wineglasses in hand. He poured himself a generous glass, then gave the bottle and extra glass to Peter.

"We can handle this," Mike said.

"How?" Peter asked, pouring himself some wine.

Mike took a quick glance at his Rolex before answering. "I've got a friend who's a PI. Give him an hour; he'll have her entire history. We'll find her. Put a quick end to this shit."

Peter took a sip and nodded.

"We'll go see him first thing tomorrow," Mike said.

"Why wait?"

"Plans."

He knew what the word meant to Mike. It was not the answer Peter wanted to hear.

"Met her at Scores the other night. Your fault for disappearing."

"Guess that answers my question."

"Oh, yeah. Dinner at the Four Seasons, then drinks back here."

Mike spread his arms wide in appreciation of the skyline. He grinned wildly in anticipation of what he'd be receiving right out on this balcony in no time at all.

All Aboard

The express train pulled in first, as it always seemed to. Mike jumped to the conclusion that it was Peter's ride.

"I'll wait for the local," he said, holding out a hand.

Peter didn't argue. He shook his agent's hand, then said, "This has to end now."

"Call me in the morning," Mike said. "I promise you, Peter, we'll take care of it. I've handled problems like this before."

Peter nodded as the local rolled into the station on the other side of the platform. Frozen in place, he watched as Mike stepped toward the car, then turned back, remembering.

"And get me a real copy of the book," Mike said, stepping into the local. "I'm dying to read the goddamn thing."

"Will do," Peter said; then, without hesitation, he turned his back on the man and stepped onto the express train.

It seemed cleaner.

Or perhaps the dirt didn't stick because of the speed.

Peter sat, staring blankly straight ahead through the window of the car. He read the advertisements. At least those were the same. The dermatologist who promised a wrinkle-free existence, the hand soap that warned of germs everywhere, the COURTESY STARTS WITH YOU sign asking riders to give up their seats to those pregnant, disabled, or old.

It chugged into the station first, the pleasant female announcer telling riders they were on a southbound number four train, next stop Grand Central. But it moved a lot slower than he would have expected. Slow enough so that the local caught up.

Peter could see directly into the other car as they rode in tandem. Mike sitting, likewise staring blankly ahead. The subway stare. The look that saves your life.

Except suddenly Mike was smiling, a look of surprise plastered to his face. He turned to speak to someone out of Peter's line of sight, someone blocked by another passenger who was standing in the way, reading the subway map.

Peter moved a little to the right and left to try to get a better view, but he couldn't tell who was making Mike smile until, satisfied he knew where he was going, the map-reading passenger moved.

And Peter realized Mike would not be smiling for long.

Unaware

He stared at the scene as if it couldn't be real. As if it were something he'd made up, written during a drunken stupor, then deleted, a cut or lost chapter from a novel he'd hopefully never have to write.

It was like watching lovers in a bar, the chemistry, the attraction, her turned-down chin matching her up-turned eyes, the soft stroke of her hair, the exaggerated laughter and smile. How could two people be so un-aware of anything else?

Peter stood, moving toward the opposite window of the car. Pressing his hands against the glass.

"That's her!!" he yelled.

But the trains were too noisy, the windows too thick.

The other riders avoided Peter; they moved away, sliding on their seats, or standing and walking to the far end. Yet no one bothered to look away. Peter was too crazed to not watch.

Banging on the window, double-fisted and hard, he tried in vain to get Mike's attention. But Mike was in his own little world.

Snapping out his cellular.

No signal.

Banging again in the hopes he could warn his friend.

That Mike might see.

But the express began to take on speed.

Peter ran toward the back of the train, pushing through the passengers who were just trying to get out of his way.

Into the next car.

But he wasn't fast enough.

The express pulled away.

Passing the local.

One last shot.

One last hard punch at the glass.

"Mike!" he yelled. "That's Dina!"

The Hard Questions

The train stopped at Grand Central Terminal.

He could run, or wait for the local.

The restaurant was on Fifty-second Street.

Looking down the line.

For a light, for a sign, for a voice telling him that a number six was pulling into the station.

There was nothing.

He could make it faster on foot.

He was sure of it.

If he didn't die first.

"Hey, this is Mike Levine. Can't answer the phone. Leave a message."

Pulling the door free, escaping onto Lexington, Peter yelled into the phone as he ran, "Mike, the girl on the subway. That's her! The girl I was telling you about."

He started catching the looks on the faces as he ran. Startled and concerned, pulling away, hiding as if he might be contagious. A deadly virus. A man no longer living, his life shattered by an indiscretion, by thoughts he should have never allowed himself to have.

Was anything worth this? Any fame, any freedom, any release? Any woman?

He should have killed her when he had the chance, he thought, running that much harder in the hopes of saving Mike's life.

The Fire

He wasn't dressed the part.

The pompous ass willing to drop four bills on dinner for two. The old khakis and a T-shirt, a hoodie pulled over for warmth. All of it old. All of it worn.

They probably thought he was there to rob the patrons. Flushed, out of breath. How long had it been since he'd shaved for Julianna?

The Four Seasons maître d' looked at him with distaste.

"May I help you, sir?" he asked. A question to which there was no answer he'd like.

Peter tried to catch a glimpse into the main dining room. He needed to see them, to see her. He'd kill her right here on the spot if he had to.

"I need to speak with Mike Levine," he explained. "It's an emergency."

The maître d' looked confused. It seemed a look he'd been practicing all of his life.

"I'm sorry, sir," he said. "Mr. Levine called and canceled his reservation for this evening. He's not here."

"That can't be," Peter said, a little too loudly, drawing looks from the more curious diners. "I just left him. He was on his way here. Are you sure?"

"Positive, sir."

Peter nodded, but he didn't move. He couldn't move. Not just yet. He needed to figure out where . . .

"Is there something else I can help you with, sir?"

Peter bolted from the restaurant, taking the stairs in a single leap, landing before a taxi, just pulling up, pushing a waiting passenger out of the way. Slamming the door shut, he barked out Mike Levine's address, telling the driver to hurry.

He never heard the cursing from the street, or the call of "Where's the goddamn fire?!"

Muzak to My Ears

The flashing lights should have tipped him off.

But he ignored them, avoided them, made no connection.

Going as far as he could in the cab, he then hightailed it on foot, past the yellow police tape, saying he was a resident to get inside. No one stopped to question him at that point. Too much excitement elsewhere.

The elevator was empty except for the sound, the piped-in soft intonations of a once-punk classic played on a harpsichord.

It actually calmed Peter a little.

And that worried him a lot.

The door to Mike's apartment was wide-open, as were the sliding glass doors leading to the deck. The blank pages of his new manuscript covered the room like giant-size confetti, as if thrown about in a fit of rage.

Dawning, realizing then, knowing it was too late, but still Peter rushed to the deck, calling out, "Mike!"

Leaning over the railing, straight down, the flashing

lights surrounding the blood-spattered white sheet. His hands gripping the rail, as if he too were about to fall. The world at that height spinning, his head throbbing. Peter's knees began to buckle just as a hand reached out to touch his shoulder.

Spinning defensively, his hands balled into fists.

A man he'd never seen before, saying, "Whoa, take it easy."

"Who are you?" Peter felt he asked.

"I was just about to ask you the same thing," the stranger said, displaying a badge.

Peter tried to focus on the name, but . . . nothing.

"Detective Gary Jessup," the stranger's voice said. "And you are . . . ?"

"Peter Robertson."

"What are you doing here, Mr. Robertson?"

Peter looked up into the detective's face at that moment. He wanted to answer his question.

If only he knew for certain.

Short For

Peter sat on the edge of Mike's sofa. He thought for a moment about how many young women had sat—or more likely, lain—on that exact same spot. How drunk or stoned or drugged, or how much were they being paid or forced? Dina, of course, being the last of them.

Did all roads lead to Dina, or just end with her?

Across from him were New York City detectives Gary Jessup and his partner, Thomas O'Reilly. One tall and thin, the other short, fat, and balding. Both in off-the-rack discount suits that had seen better days. One asked questions to which no answer seemed right; his ponderous grunts said as much. The other took notes, spoke to his partner as if he were the only other person in the room, and sipped coffee from an old travel mug. Neither would win awards for style or diction.

Peter finished telling his story.

". . . as soon as I realized he'd canceled his dinner reservations," he said, staring at the paper bag on the coffee table before him. The top of the one remaining bottle of wine peeking through reminded him that he'd forgotten it there. That he was so late getting back. Would she start to suspect? Would she . . . ?

"Can you verify any of this?" Jessup asked.

"I'll call the restaurant," O'Reilly said, standing, walking toward the balcony, already on his cellular.

"Look. I came here because she switched the manuscript to my new book," Peter explained.

"Right," Jessup said, holding the box cover in his hand. " 'Be careful what you wish for . . .' " he read off Peter's note. "Sounds almost like a threat."

Peter stared at the man as if he couldn't believe what he was hearing. It was a joke, a little sarcasm. A manuscript long overdue. One that Mike might not have been ready to read, let alone sell. It certainly had taken its toll on Peter.

"Mike was my friend."

"So you've said."

"Look," Peter said, raising his voice. "I'm sure the maître d' at the Four Seasons will remember me."

"He does," O'Reilly said, returning, looking at his partner. "That part of this story checks out."

"Huh," Jessup said. "What about the girl . . . ?" He glanced up at O'Reilly for a name.

"Dina."

"Do you know anything about her other than her first name?"

Peter let a small blast of air escape his lungs. "We . . . um . . . were staying at the same place in Madison. That was"—he gave it some thought, trying to recall for how long now his life had been uprooted—"two weeks ago tonight."

"Her room number?"

Peter shook his head. "Wouldn't know."

He had never seen her room.

"And no address for her in New York, no phone number? Nothing?"

He looked first at Jessup, then at O'Reilly. He thought about telling them everything, but what if it got back to Julianna? He couldn't risk that. Though he already had.

Peter lied instead, or stretched the truth. As far as he now knew, her phone and address had changed. He shook his head again as his only response.

"We can get a list of every incoming call to his apartment over the last couple of weeks," O'Reilly said.

Jessup nodded, then asked, "You said you and your wife have a daughter?"

"Yes, sir," Peter replied, "Kimberly."

"If this woman was harassing you, why didn't you report it? Weren't you concerned about the safety of your family?"

The question caught Peter off guard. Why hadn't he? he wondered now. Why had he let it get to this? To save his marriage and his family was the easy answer, but perhaps that was what he was risking most.

"I . . . didn't think . . . she was . . . dangerous."

"You thought she was dangerous enough to warn Mr. Levine," Jessup pointed out.

"I guess," Peter said. "Yes."

"Huh," he said. Then: "Were you having an affair with Ms. Bailey?"

Peter pictured that kiss, the only kiss really, in the doorway to his Madison hotel room. He could feel her hands on his body as if they'd never left. As if she'd never stopped. As if he'd do it all over again, given the chance.

But he wouldn't. He was so sure of that now.

"What sort of question is that?" Peter asked.

"An obvious one," O'Reilly interjected.

Peter shot the detective a look. Disdainful and angry, wishing he could understand his motives. "No," he said. "I was not having an affair with her."

"Huh," Jessup said again. "Dina . . ."

"What about her?"

"That short for anything? A nickname?"

Peter shrugged. "It means 'God has judged,'" he said.

"You don't say."

"I had an aunt once named Dina," O'Reilly said, suddenly rambling. "Didn't find out until she died that her real name was Geraldine."

Peter glanced over at the cop.

"The priest kept going on about 'May the soul of Geraldine O'Reilly rest in peace,'" O'Reilly continued. "'May the souls of all the faithful departed rest in—'"

"Christ!" Peter muttered, cutting into the detective's story as he sat back on the sofa. Shaking his head as if a missing puzzle piece had just fallen into place, and he could finally see the bigger picture.

"'. . . peace.' I thought I was at the wrong goddamn funeral," O'Reilly concluded. "Had to ask my mother who the fuck was Geraldine."

"Geraldine is Angel," Peter explained.

The cops shared a glance, then looked over. It was Jessup who asked, "Angel?"

"It was mentioned only once in the first book," Peter said, "how she was named after her"—he nodded an acknowledgment at O'Reilly—"aunt Geraldine, and she hated the name. She made everyone call her Angel. That was her father's nickname for her. So it stuck."

"Slow down a minute. Who's Angel?"

"The lead character of my first book, Angel Bailey. Her real name is Geraldine Bailey. And that's the name she goes back to using in my new book, so no one will know who she is."

Peter could picture the first time they met, standing in the lobby of the Willy Street Playhouse. Dina held the first edition in her hand. "That's me," she had told him. "This book is me."

"The missing book?" Jessup asked, placing a hand squarely atop the empty manuscript box.

Nodding, Peter continued, "Dina was obsessed with this character. She knew the book by heart."

He pictured the name on the buzzer to her apartment: G. BAILEY. At the time so damn confusing. He never thought of Dina as a nickname for Geraldine.

"Fuck!" Peter said. "Now I realize even her name—"

O'Reilly cut him off. "You sure we're talking about a real person here? This Dina?"

"Yes, Detective, I'm very sure. Her name is Bailey. Geraldine Bailey."

The cops weren't buying it. O'Reilly stepped aside and barked into his walkie-talkie, "See what you can find on a Geraldine Bailey." He looked over at Peter. "How old? What's she look like?"

"Twenty-one," he replied. "Short, maybe five-two. Slender. Black hair. Green eyes."

"Good memory," Jessup said, shooting him a suspicious glance, as O'Reilly repeated her description into the walkie.

"She looked just like Angel, all grown-up," Peter explained. "Pretty easy for me to describe."

"Do you have a copy of this book, *Angel*?"

"I can give you one right now," Peter said, standing.

He walked over to Mike's elaborate glass-doored built-in shelves. Opening one of the doors to the case where the books of Mike's clients were all arranged, alphabetically by author, he reached in, and . . .

"That's strange."

"What's strange?" Jessup asked.

Peter stared at the empty space on the bookshelf where Mike's signed copy of *Angel* should be. Just a space now. An inch and a half wide. Nothing more.

As if the book were never there to begin with.

"It's gone," Peter said, trying to remember if he'd noticed it earlier, or if perhaps in a rage that Peter had dropped him as his agent, Mike had thrown the book away. Turning, he found the two detectives standing right behind him.

"Huh," Jessup said, shooting his partner a look. "Ain't that always the way?"

More Excuses

It made sense.

He wasn't in the system.

Despite what should have been a record as long as her arm. Despite what should have been arrests and convictions. Despite what should have been a life behind bars, the key long disposed of. Not a three-time loser—a lifetime loser.

Despite, despite, despite.

She lit up, sucking in the smoke, letting it fill her lungs, letting it carry her away.

So good they ought to be illegal, she thought, still staring at the printout, a fingerprint analysis. Easy to print a dead man.

Even better when cold cases were allowed to thaw.

Another drag, her head pressing back against her chair, eyeing the ever-spreading stain of yellow on the ceiling tiles over her desk.

Your lungs on Camels.

She couldn't get the phrase *ten-point match* out of her head. It was dream, a slam dunk. Ten points got you convictions, with nothing overturned on appeal. Ten points was twenty to life, hard time, Sing Sing.

Ten points was a needle in the arm.

Easy to sentence a dead man to death.

Letting go of another drag, Rossi let out a long, low whistle.

If that wasn't all the motive in the world, all the motive anyone would ever need, she just didn't know what was.

The Note

He'd been gone too long.

Peter entered his apartment to discover a note on the fridge.

Pulling it from beneath the silver dog-bone magnet always used for such things, he read:

Gone to the store.
Taking Groucho along for the ride. Be back soon.
Love ya.

He held the small bright yellow slip of paper for a moment, then placed it back under the magnet on the refrigerator door.

"I still have time," he muttered.

Wondering if that was the plan all along.

If she couldn't have him, she'd destroy him. Make him seem the crazy one, unstable, everything in his fucking head.

Even his goddamn book.

Eye level. The bookshelf in his office. The copies of every edition, mint and clean and—

Gone.

The shelves empty, except for the tracks of dust, as if the books had been removed, recently and in too much of a rush to bother cleaning up.

She'd been there again.

Peter knew it. Backing away from the shelf, he could feel her, smell her trail of deceit.

Waking his computer, Peter clicked on the desktop icon for *It's a Wonderful Lie.* The title, *A novel by Peter Robertson,* scrolling down, the pages . . .

Blank.

He could feel the tightness again. The air not coming. He needed to sit, to stop, but . . . Pulling open a top desk drawer, a box of computer disks, backups, he always kept backups everywhere, finding a floppy marked with the words: *First Novel* X-ed out, replaced by *Angel.*

Popping it into the drive, searching the disk.

"Fuck!"

The words all too clear: DISK EMPTY.

Ripping through drawers now, ripping through his apartment, the firebox on the top shelf of their bedroom closet, all for other backups, popping them in, one after another in sweaty disbelief.

Nothing.

No files.

No novel.

No Angel.

The Search

Barnes & Noble on Astor Place was the closest.

Peter rushed through the shelves of fiction, finding what should have been his section, between Nora Roberts and James Rollins. *Angel* had been a best-seller. The paperback reprinted a dozen times. It was a stock item.

Always in fucking stock.

Except today.

At the information desk he asked.

"I'm looking for a book called *Angel*," he said. "The author's name is Peter Robertson."

The young woman behind the desk punched some keys on her computer. She looked at him and spelled out his last name.

"Yes," he said expectantly. "That's right."

"I'm sorry," she said. "I have a few books listed here titled *Angel*, but none by that author."

"But it has to be there," he said.

"Is it new?" she asked.

"No."

"Out of print, perhaps?"

"No."

"I'm sorry."

Nodding, more to himself, hating himself for what he had done, what he had allowed her to do, he ran west, picking up speed, shortness of breath no longer an issue; he didn't need to breathe. Turning the corner, heading south on Broadway—he'd done a signing at Shakespeare & Co. He and Julianna had gone out for drinks with the manager and his wife.

The book had been featured on the new-release table long after it had been a new release.

They would have *Angel* in stock.

But the empty space suggested otherwise.

Now starting to feel as if he were being followed, watched, as if Dina were there, he ran south to Bleecker and hung a right, over to Village Books. They always had a good half dozen copies in stock. He was always getting a call to swing by and sign the book whenever new copies arrived.

But today there were no copies.

Ripping the other books from the shelves.

Wanting to tear down the goddamn shelves.

"It's got to be here," he yelled. "It's supposed to be right fucking here."

Customer Satisfaction

She found Juicy seated in the kitchen, a barely touched can of Coke on the table in front of her, her eyes puffy from crying, whatever fingernails she might once have had long past the help of any manicurist.

"Something wrong with the Coke?" Rossi said.

"I hate Coke," Juicy said. "Fucking cop said I couldn't have a beer. I wasn't old enough."

"Funny where some men will draw the line," she said.

"Yeah, hysterical," Juicy said.

Rossi backed away, opened the fridge door, and pulled out a bottle of imported pale ale. She twisted off the top, took a seat opposite Juicy, then slid the bottle down on the tabletop, slid it across the expanse. Juicy snatched it up, took a swig, then slammed it back down, wiping the foam off her mouth with the back of her hand.

If ever anyone looked like they needed a drink, the detective thought, but instead said, "Mind if I smoke?"

"Fair trade-off," Juicy said, then, "Can I have one?"

"Your lungs," Rossi said, shrugging, jiggling the

package so that a Camel popped its head from the hole. She lit Juicy's first, then her own.

She loved that first drag.

"Did Raoul ever have contact with someone named Peter Robertson?" she asked.

Instead of answering, Juicy took another swig from the bottle.

"Do you know Peter Robertson?"

Nothing.

"Juicy?"

The answer came this time. Quietly. "Yeah, I saw him once."

"How did Raoul know him?"

More silence. Her turn for a long drag.

"Juicy?"

"Why should I tell you any of this shit?"

"So I can arrest the person who did this."

"Like you really care," Juicy said, her eyes suddenly flooded with tears.

"Peter Robertson?" Rossi asked again.

"Yeah. Yeah. Raoul told him shit for that book of his."

"*Angel?*"

Juicy nodded, sniffled, then stood. She walked through the passageway into the living room, reaching up to the top shelf of Raoul's bookshelf.

"He signed it to Raoul and all," she explained.

Something stopped her short.

"Huh?"

"What's wrong?"

"It's gone," Juicy said.

"The book?"

"It was here the other day. I looked at it after he left."

"Peter Robertson was here recently?"

"Yeah. On business."

"What kind of business, Juicy?"

"Raoul business," she said. "Not my business."

"There any difference?"

"I don't get involved with Raoul's other shit."

"But you know what Peter was here for?"

"I'm not deaf," Juicy said, shaking her head, not that it mattered anymore. "He was looking to buy a gun."

"And did he?"

Juicy gave a sad little laugh that seemed aged beyond her years. "You work for Raoul and you learn one thing."

"What's that?" Rossi asked.

"Always keep the customer satisfied," she said.

Man of Action

He didn't know where they'd gone. Where she'd gone. It was as if his life were disappearing before his eyes. His novel, Dina. Was this the punishment for his sin? To erase what he dreamed of, what took him so long to create? Or was she just taking possession of his work, taking it with her to the other side?

His hands were shaking as he locked the dead bolt behind him. Checking it to make sure. Thinking he needed to have it replaced. He needed more locks. He needed bars on his windows.

"Julianna, you home yet?" he called out.

But looking around he saw there were still no signs of life. Just the note on the fridge door, exactly where he'd left it.

"Good," he said, receiving no answer. "I can take care of this."

Taking a seat before his computer, Peter took a deep breath; then, with his hands shaking even worse now, he very slowly typed an A, then an N, then a G, an E.

The middle finger of his right hand hovered over the L as if it were a panic button, red, deadly, nuclear annihilation. He pressed it firmly. But instead of the letter he expected, the conclusion to her name, the half word *Ange* disappeared from the screen.

Blink.

Staring at the monitor, wondering if his eyes were playing tricks now, Peter repeated the action, a little faster this time, slapping down the keys with determination.

But the outcome was the same.

He tried D-I-N, but the A acted as some hyperbackspace, deleting the other three letters.

"Son of a bitch," he muttered.

He tried her last name, B-A-I-L-E, his fingers typing as fast as they possibly could. But as soon as he hit the Y her name disappeared.

Sitting back in his chair, he felt as if the walls to his office were suddenly closing in on him. Even his desk, shrinking before his eyes. The Virgin Mary rolling down like a window shade in reverse.

Everything got smaller, except for his computer. The monitor expanded, taking over the room, as if it were the only thing he would ever need to see.

"What the fuck are you doing?" he asked.

His answer came on the monitor, the words typing themselves where he had just tried to write her name: *I don't exist*, was written. *I never have*.

His own words thrown back. Slamming Dina against the wall in her apartment, holding her face. So close to strangling the life from her.

"As far as I'm concerned," he had told her, "you

don't exist. You never have. Killing you would mean nothing to me."

If only he were a man of action.

Instead of a man of words.

Questions

Lewis Street. A stone's throw from the Williamsburg Bridge. One of the few blocks on this island not yet gentrified.

Rossi found comfort in knowing there were still slums in Manhattan. That the yuppies hadn't taken over completely. Not yet, anyway.

Pushing her way into a foyer she'd never consider entering if not armed, she maneuvered her way past piss stains and debris, rap music and screaming kids, to the second floor, where she knocked on the door to apartment 2-A.

"I'm coming," came the female voice from the other side, a slight street twang to her pronunciation.

Waiting, Rossi thought about the circumstances that delivered us to our godforsaken evils. Were we all just victims with varying expense accounts? Were we all just fucked?

The woman answered, dressed in an out-of-style jeans skirt and a faded New York Yankees T-shirt that looked a few sizes too small. The bags under her eyes, the leathery complexion of her skin made her look at least a decade older than her twenty or so years. The frizziness of her hair didn't help.

She might have been pretty once, Rossi thought.

"What?" the woman demanded.

Rossi flipped open her badge case. "Lucinda Young?" she asked.

It took a moment. Attitude. Not someone who disliked badges; someone who was frightened of them.

"Yeah," Lucinda said tentatively.

"Could I ask you a couple of questions?"

"I guess that would depend what they're about," Lucinda said.

"Raoul Santiago," came Rossi's reply.

Lucinda's eyes drifted to the ceiling. Her jaw twisted and locked in an annoyed grimace. Yet despite the hardness, she looked as if she were about to cry.

"Only if you're here to tell me that motherfucker's dead," she said, holding back the tears.

Lucinda had long ago promised herself she'd shed her last tear for that bastard.

Gone Forever

He stared at the words as they appeared letter by letter on his computer screen: *Even you can't bring me back now.*

"Just watch me," Peter said.

He typed furiously, mouthing the words to the opening paragraph of his novel, words Dina could recite from memory, as he banged the keys.

She put the lipstick on last, amused that it was always what would come off first, before even the most obvious stitch of clothing. On lips sometimes, or a cheek, or less likely a starched white collar. But usually, at least half the time, it found its way elsewhere, a marking, well-charted territory, a bright red macho cock-ring tattoo.

He sat back, stared at the monitor, waiting for something to happen.

But nothing did.

Just the words on the page. His words. She could never take them from him.

Leaning forward, he began the next paragraph, a paragraph whose first sentence started with her name, Angel.

His finger hit the A key.

Nothing.

He hit it again, harder.

Still nothing.

Again, and again, and again.

Nothing.

Screaming at the computer, Peter lifted the keyboard off the desk, slamming it back down. Jamming the A key with the middle finger of his left hand. Punching the goddamn key.

But still nothing.

Sitting back, furious and frightened, glaring at the screen. Peter's face suddenly blanched. He felt ill, lost, alone, as every word he typed, those three sentences he had once written and rewritten until he could smell them in his dreams, disappeared from the screen.

One letter at a time.

Rossi

Perhaps there are no fictions, Rossi thought as she stepped from Lucinda's building and answered her cellular on the second ring.

"Rossi," she said softly, her mind wandering on to, *Where could we have all gone so wrong?* Weren't the most deviant, most heinous just a reflection of society at large? To what end would our pleasures supercede decency, common or otherwise? To what end would we stop?

So wrong.

The question on the other end of the line snapped her back. Along with it a name she should have been expecting.

Right at the top of her list.

"Yeah, I'm on my way over there now," she said. "Why?"

The answer on the other end of the line brought an angry curse and the immediate need to light up.

PART FIVE

PART FIVE

Angel

It was a cleansing.

Baptism by fire.

To destroy any reminder of her old life, any reminder of him, was to destroy her old life, was to destroy him.

Wide sweeps at first. A slash through the Jackson Pollock mess that had been her wardrobe, clothes designed not for comfort, not clothes she even liked. The sexy, the short, the push-up, the spiked, some fantasies she'd never understand. It had never mattered before, part of the role. Playing a part. Answering to the desires of others. Never her own. Never.

But with each slash, the anger intensified. The intensity magnified. Specifics. Buttons, zippers—she became fixated on what they'd pull open, the easy access made available. She could feel the hands on her. How many goddamn hands? She could smell their sweat, hear their fucking grunts of joy.

Pulling at the seams, the material, made to be loved, not detested, ripping like a child. Ripping as she did, every time. Every time lately. When it was no longer her decision. Was it ever her decision? Yes, she wanted to believe at first that it was. She needed to. She could never be that much of a victim. That pathetic. She didn't buy the excuse that she was only a child. She answered his goddamn ad. She liked the cash; she liked the sex.

Crying, the thought that she had once liked the sex.

"Fuck!" she screamed.

Scissors in hands now, cutting, ripping, snapping. A face for every boiling tear, the cash changing hands, changing, exchanging. What had she done with her life?

Pulling paintings from her bedroom walls, jewelry from her night table drawers, shiny trinkets of gold and diamonds, meant to be worn in their company. Gifts, they'd all been gifts in exchange for the pleasures she'd provided.

Slicing into the bed next, its sheets and silk comforter so stained with the pressure of submission and hopelessness. Reaching deep into the mattress, slicing off its gills, gutting it of heart and lungs, chopping off its head.

If only she could do that to the men who treated her like a toy borrowed from the kid who lived down the street.

The one they made fun of behind his back.

Peter

Peter finally understood with clarity his own words, as he brought the walls to his office crashing down.

Realism

"Hey, Rossi, how's it shaking?"

The thin air at this altitude robbed her of what little nicotine rush the cigarette on the ride up to Midtown east provided.

"Same old shit, O'Reilly," she said, taking in the splendor of Mike Levine's apartment, feeling as much out of place as the two detectives in front of her looked, like a bum in Armani. Being on this job long enough made one beyond dressing up. "I need a smoke."

"I doubt the owner will mind," O'Reilly replied.

Rossi didn't need any more permission.

"This is my partner, Gary Jessup," O'Reilly said, then nodded at Rossi. "Rossi here's an old friend from the academy."

"Yeah," she replied in a tone that made Jessup want to change the subject, "Thomas and I go way back."

Jessup didn't let the uncomfortable click of silence take hold. "What's this about our vic tying into Halliwell?" he asked.

"Ever read a book called *Angel*?" Rossi asked.

Jessup shot his partner a look.

"Heard of it," O'Reilly said.

"There really such a book?" Jessup said.

Nodding, sucking in a drag that could collapse a lung, Rossi explained, "It's about a young girl who thinks she's invincible. She gets sucked into prostitution, then drugs, and ends up being pimped out by a dealer in Alphabet City."

"Realistic?"

"Let's just say the details cut a little too close to the truth," she replied.

Lucinda (Part Two)

"Raoul was pissed. I never saw him mad like that before. He beat me with his fists. Asked me over and over again what I told him. But I said I didn't tell Peter nothing." She shook her head in anger. "Raoul said Peter made him look like a fool. Like some young girl could outsmart him. I tried to tell him that it wasn't about him, that it was just a book, fake, fiction, but Raoul wouldn't listen. He didn't care about no fiction. I don't even think he knew what the word meant. The only thing he knew was that Peter needed to be taught a lesson."

Rossi sat across from Lucinda at a small kitchen table taking notes. As the young woman spoke, the detective looked about the apartment. It was clean, organized, with small feminine touches that made it feel homey, despite its location.

"Did Peter ever touch you?"

"No, ma'am," Lucinda said. "The only man who never did."

"Your father?" Rossi asked.

No reply came. From the look on Lucinda's face, stoic but regretful, from the way she let the breath escape her lungs, obviously none was needed.

"How'd Raoul get the car?" Rossi asked.

"I guess that's where I came in," Lucinda replied. "He'd had enough of me."

"Meaning?"

"He said he needed the Escalade." She shrugged. "They reported the car jacked, but he really just gave it to him, got me in return. I became their own private little whore until they got sick of me." She shook her head, clenching her jaw at the memory. "An even trade."

"They?" Rossi asked, looking at her, wondering how much she once looked like the Angel in Peter's novel. "You mean Jeffrey Halliwell?"

"Yeah, him and Mike."

Rossi could hear the name coming out of her mouth before she even said it.

"Levine? Peter's agent?"

"I think that was his last name, yes. Jeff was driving. Mike was the passenger. The witness. Who was gonna argue with that?"

No one, Rossi thought, *after what happened.*

"Did they know what Raoul was going to do with the Escalade?" she asked.

"Don't think they cared," Lucinda said. "I think they were pretty happy with the trade-off."

Rossi let that sit.

"Did you ever tell Peter about any of this?"

But instead of answering, Lucinda let out another gasp of air, this one compact, and looked away.

Rossi was sure she saw Lucinda's eyes filling with tears.

The young woman found it easy to still cry for Peter Robertson.

No Longer in Reverse

It had been a good morning.

The best in Peter's life.

Angel *was in the top spot on* The New York Times Book Review *best-seller list.*

Awaking from a nap on the sofa, one that seemed to come naturally during a Mets game, he found his family gone, all explained in a note held by a dog-bone magnet on the refrigerator door.

Groceries, most likely.

The health food store Julianna so loved on the Upper West Side.

Throwing on a clean shirt, and needing to wake up so he could return the congratulatory calls, Peter walked two blocks for a cup of coffee.

It was a gorgeous day.

Traffic was light.

They were two blocks away from home, waiting for the light to change, when Julianna spotted him and pointed.

"Look! There's Daddy."

She sat behind the wheel of their old red Saab, sending her

*husband the warmest of smiles. Kimberly was in the back-
seat, right behind her. She was waving. Groucho sat on the
seat next to Kimberly, his head half leaning out the window,
oblivious to all but the sun. Two bags of groceries were on the
floor in front of the front passenger seat.*

*Peter waved back, happy to see them. He pointed at the cof-
fee shop, motioning that he'd pick up a latte for her as well.*

*Julianna gave him a thumbs-up, just as a horn bellowed to
her left.*

Someone yelled, "The light's green, asshole!"

*Neither she nor her husband turned to notice the black
Cadillac Escalade stopped at a green light, generating the
wrath of those drivers behind it. The driver wiped the sweat
from his brow, raised the hood of his hoodie, then glared over
to his right at the red Saab Julianna was driving.*

Her light changed from red to green.

*She pressed the accelerator slowly, moving into the inter-
section.*

The driver of the Escalade gunned it.

*Peter's warm smile morphed into a holocaust. He stopped
waving, his hand frozen in front of his face, watching as the
bodies in his car snapped forward and back like rag dolls as
the Cadillac chrome burst through the red door, through the
glass, almost cutting the car in half.*

The explosion crashed like God's fist.

Loud.

Panicked screeches surrounded them.

And the sound of life flittering away.

*The driver beat at the Cadillac's air bag, pulling himself
from the wreckage through the open window. Standing on
shaky legs, running away from the smoke, the screams, the
carnage. Shaking, hurt, falling against a light post. Holding
on to it. His fingers ripping into the metal.*

Frozen, not yet able to move, Peter watched one of the Saab's hubcaps, flashing silver and grime, roll down the street.

It stopped at the foot of a man in a hoodie, fell and lay flat on worn gray asphalt.

Looking up, Peter caught the man's eyes for a second.

He knew the man.

He'd never forget his smirk.

Initial Reaction

"Lucinda told me this was about a year ago," Rossi said. "*Angel* was on the best-seller list, and suddenly Raoul's masculinity felt compromised. He gives her up for the car."

"And takes his rage out on Robertson's wife and kid," Jessup said, shaking his head in disgust.

"Right," Rossi said, nodding. "Then shortly after the accident Peter had a nervous breakdown, checked himself into an institution."

"What the fuck's he doing out?" Jessup asked.

"Yeah," O'Reilly agreed. "He was just talking about his wife and daughter like they were alive."

"When you check yourself in, you can check yourself out," she said.

"You seem to know a lot about this guy," O'Reilly said.

"I was one of his sources on the book," she explained. "I met him when he was a reporter for the *Times*."

"Never knew that," O'Reilly said, as if he felt injured being kept out of Rossi's loop.

"No one did." She shrugged. "Since he got out, he's been going to his daughter's school every day, like he has to pick her up. I got a call on it, but . . . he just walks over, sits for a while, watches all the other kids leave, then goes home. What are we gonna do, lock him up for that?"

Before O'Reilly or Jessup could respond, a call came from the kitchen of Mike's apartment. One of the forensic techs who looked like he could have still been in high school said, "Detectives, I think you'll want to see this."

They followed him over to a slide-out trash compartment, made to look like any other kitchen cabinet in the room. The white plastic basket was lined with a fresh white plastic bag. The only contents a silver stiletto blade, which had left a track of blood on its way to the bottom of the bin.

With a rubber-gloved hand, the techie retrieved the blade, displaying it for the detectives before dropping it into an evidence bag.

"Those markings?" O'Reilly asked.

"Initials," Rossi said, adding sadly, "P. R."

"You sure?"

"Yeah," she said, heading for the door. "I remember seeing the damn thing on his desk when he interviewed me for the book."

Reality Hits Home

The door to Peter's apartment creaked open at the slightest touch.

All three cops drew their weapons, hurriedly stepping through the doorway into Peter's kitchen. The stench of rotten food and filth assaulted their senses. Used take-out cartons, now nothing more than half-opened petri dishes, moldy and vile, lined the countertops covered in mildew and grime. The doors of the kitchen cabinets hung tentatively on broken hinges, as if ripped off in a rage. The toaster looked as if it had been set on fire.

The floor was littered with broken cabinet drawers and utensils, balled-up paper towels, and crumpled coffee cups. Two ceramic dog bowls sat off in one corner, one cracked down the middle, the other stained with dried pieces of food and a dead cockroach on its back.

Rossi stood in front of the fridge, reading the note from Julianna, so faded, so dirty, so brittle around the edges, as if looked at and touched a thousand times.

Last words, she thought.

* * *

The living room was filthy, the dining room table stacked high with pizza boxes and fast-food wrappers, empty bottles of bourbon and wine. Newspapers covered the stained fabric of the sofa, napkins and paper coffee cups, and toys, so many of Kimberly's toys, strewn about as if a whirlwind had struck. A child's desk, broken, as if someone had fallen onto it.

And on top of it all, surrounding the mass, hundreds of copies of Peter's book *Angel*. Stacks of the book, falling over. Some still in plastic bags from Barnes & Noble, Shakespeare & Co., every other bookstore in New York. Piled onto the sofa, in the trash. Thrown carelessly, scattershot.

O'Reilly picked up one of the copies of *Angel*, opening it, noticing the handwritten inscription: *Mike, All because of you, Peter.*

"What the hell is going on?" Jessup asked.

"We're in Disney World," came an answer of sorts from the TV, where the family vacation video played, happiness in all its glory, not always what it was cracked up to be.

Gone

His cry came from down the hall.

"Why are you doing this?"

They rushed toward the sound, needing to push their way against the debris into his office. Finding him leaning over his computer, staring hopelessly at the monitor, now blank.

With one hand holding a crumpled ball of paper and the other buried deep in his jacket pocket, Peter rocked back and forth slightly, repeating one word over and over again.

"Why?"

He never noticed them behind him, holstering their weapons, taking in the damage he had inflicted. Nothing remained on the shelves, on the walls; it was as if he'd whipped the room with a pickax, leaving not even a shadow standing.

"Peter?" Rossi said quietly, coming up behind him.

"She's gone."

"Who, Peter?" Rossi asked. "Who's gone?"

It took a moment for him to answer, but when he finally did the name sounded a million miles away.

"Dina," he said.

Dina and Halliwell
(Revised Chapter)

It was easier than he expected.

He thought nothing of the call. It was as if Peter were an old friend welcomed into his home with a bottle of wine. A *good* bottle of wine. A 1964 Palmer Bordeaux.

Perhaps Jeffrey Halliwell was softening.

We all did with age.

"What can I do for you this time?" he asked.

They were standing in the living room, having just clinked their glasses together in cheers. Peter explained he was working on a sequel, and this was part of his research.

"I never read the first book," Halliwell admitted. "No offense. I just don't have time to read."

"None taken," Peter replied.

"What's this one about?" Halliwell asked.

"Revenge," Peter said.

"And how can I help with that?" Halliwell said, a little confused.

Peter's explanation was sudden.

Halliwell gasped, with a hard blink.

He tried to speak, but only a click of sorts escaped his lips.

Taking a rough step back, his hand slamming down on the closest table, knocking the bottle of Bordeaux to the floor, he looked down at the handle protruding from the chest. Silver, a little tarnished, with worn swirls and the initials P.R.

Peter gave the handle a good tug and pulled the long blade free, taking with it a streak of Halliwell's blood.

Finishing off the glass of wine, he watched Halliwell drop to his knees and die.

"That's how," he said.

Peter, Raoul, and Dina
(Revised Chapter)

"You alone?" Peter asked.

"Why do you need to know that?"

"Because I'd like to talk to you," he replied, "for the new book."

"What?" Raoul asked. "You wanna get it right this time?"

"Something like that."

Raoul shook his head and laughed. He walked toward the kitchen, opening the fridge, leaning in.

"You know everything that little cunt Lucinda told you was wrong?" he said, pulling out two longneck bottles.

"No," Peter said, right behind him, bashing down on the side of Raoul's head with the butt of the Beretta. "She was right about a few things."

Dragging the stunned man into the bedroom, Peter handcuffed Raoul's hands to the footboard over his head. Then, kneeling close, he slapped him awake, holding his face with one hand so Peter could see into Raoul's terrified eyes.

"What are you, fucking crazy?" Raoul yelled.

As an answer, Peter scratched the blade of the stiletto across the whiskers on Raoul's face.

"What do you want? You can have anything. Just take it."

"Thank you," Peter said, sliding the stiletto slowly into Raoul's chest, until none of the blade could be seen. "I will."

Blow Jobs and Balconies
(Revised Chapter)

"I saw her go into your office today," Peter said, sitting back on the sofa, spotting the bag of wine bottles on Mike's coffee table. How long had it been since he'd been home?

Mike was barely paying attention. "Oh, yeah, when?"

"Right after I dropped off the manuscript."

"Really?" he said.

"Yeah, why?"

"Well . . ."

Mike stepped to his kitchen, returning a second later with Peter's boxed manuscript. He tossed the box onto the coffee table in front of his client.

". . . that would explain this?"

Peter looked at him for a beat, then leaned forward and opened it. The cover page was as it should be.

The rest was not.

Mike pulled one of the bottles from the paper bag. He made a face as he read the label, but opened it anyway. "I thought it was your way of telling me to piss off."

Not exactly, Peter thought, the weight of his anger crushing as he stepped out onto the deck for air. If only it were that easy.

Mike was right behind him, glass of wine in hand. Though it was Peter's bottle, he offered him none.

"You can handle this," Mike said, turning to stare out at his view. A view that reminded him of a recent hookup with a blue-eyed blonde in black.

Moving closer to his friend, Peter gave him a hearty pat on the shoulder with his left hand, as his right stabbed up suddenly into Mike's throat with the stiletto, and with one shove Mike was over the railing.

"I know I can," Peter said.

The Truth

"She took Angel with her."

As Rossi glanced back at Jessup and O'Reilly, Peter turned, noticing them for the first time. He nodded toward them.

"I told them all about her," he said. "In Mike's apartment. She's the one who killed him, and Raoul." His voice dropped off. "And Halliwell."

"How did you know Raoul was dead?" Jessup asked.

"He has to be," Peter replied matter-of-factly. "The deadline has passed."

"What deadline?"

"My promise to Kimberly," he explained. "Dina made sure I didn't break that promise."

O'Reilly held out a copy of the book he'd picked up in the other room. He displayed the cover to Peter.

"Is this Dina?" he asked.

It was like seeing a long-lost friend. He never meant to hurt her. To frighten her.

He never meant for her to go away.

"Where did you find that?" Peter said, elated. "I thought she made them all disappear."

"She's not real, Peter," Rossi said, watching him as he laid a crumpled sheet of paper on the desk, flattening out the wrinkles with one hand.

Noticing the letterhead.

A past-due bill for the burial of his wife and child, on beige linen stock, in a very serious font.

Peter looked down for a moment, reading the words yet again.

"She is to me," he said.

Past Due

He stood before their coffins.

A minister spoke, the words a blur, a shambles in his head. Something about all the faithful departed and the mercy of God. Something about resting in peace.

Glancing over the coffins at the people paying their respects. So many people he barely knew.

At front and center stood Mike.

Beside him was Lucinda, nursing a black eye and visibly upset. Mike put his arm around her, as if to offer comfort, and whispered into her ear. She froze and pulled away just slightly, as far away as she could, hardly comforted.

To her other side, like a guard—or an owner, Peter thought—was Jeffrey Halliwell, who simply looked bored. Too important to mourn.

And next to him, Raoul.

He glared at Peter, a smirk playing on his face.

The same smirk.

The accident.

Not an accident at all.

He could picture Raoul now, bloodied, standing by the

light pole, lowering his shades and turning to look for Peter's reaction.

Locking eyes for just a beat before Peter turned to see the car, so recognizable now. Halliwell's Escalade.

Before Peter ran to try to save his family.

But now was not the time.

The time would come.

Peter nodded at them, all three, then looked back down at the coffins, allowing himself to be buried with Julianna and Kimberly in his grief.

Madison (Revised Chapter)

The doctors joked that the sign for the hospital could be seen from outer space.

THE MADISON PSYCHIATRIC INSTITUTE, in bold red letters against a white background, propped on the lawn in front of a generic bore of a building, set on the corner of Willy Street and Playhouse Road, across from a Best Western Hotel in the sticks of Wisconsin.

Peter sat at a table by the window, staring out blankly at the institute sign. He was dressed in his usual attire, a bathrobe and slippers. He clutched a book to his chest with his left hand, while gnawing the thumbnail of his right, wondering when he started chewing his nails.

He couldn't remember.

"Excuse me, Mr. Robertson," came a soft, pretty voice.

Peter looked up as a young trainee placed a flyer down on the table in front of him. The girl was blond and a little pudgy.

"We're showing a movie tonight, right after dinner," she said.

Peter nodded, then looked down at the flyer. It showed a photo of the actor Jimmy Stewart grinning broadly, surrounded by family. It was for the film It's a Wonderful Life.

Peter took his book and placed it down on the table near the flyer. It was his first edition of Angel. *The girl on the cover looked like no one he knew.*

Turning then to look at the other patients in the institute, he caught the eye of his friend Sam Friedman, a burly man with Einstein hair and a goofy grin, who'd been in Madison his entire life. Sam was decorating a Christmas tree with Tony Rialto, a patient whom Peter secretly disliked, and an older woman named Clara.

Sam waved back, pointed at the tree, and yelled "therapeutical." Then he laughed loudly.

Everything was therapeutic to Sam.

Peter looked back up at the trainee.

But she seemed different, sublime now, sharp-edged and radical. With jet-black hair ringing her oval face.

She seemed familiar.

Looking down at the cover to his book, then back up into her face, he asked, "Are you Angel?"

The trainee smiled and spoke in a comforting voice. "Yes, I'm an angel."

Peter nodded, looked down again at the book and the movie flyer for a moment, then back out the window at the Madison sign.

It was all beginning to make sense.

It's a Wonderful Lie

"I've heard enough," Jessup said, impatiently pulling Peter to his feet.

"Where are you taking me?" Peter protested, pulling the Beretta from his pocket, taking aim at Jessup's head. "I need to be here in case she comes back."

The cops froze, their hands out, trying to calm him down.

"Put the gun down, Peter," Rossi yelled.

"She's not coming back," O'Reilly said.

"You don't believe me, do you?" Peter asked, stepping back against the closest wall, watching them all, but glaring at Jessup.

"No, sir," the detective said. "I do not."

"Try to type her name," Peter ordered, nodding toward the computer. "She won't let you."

Jessup didn't move.

"Peter!"

"Do it!"

Glaring back, Jessup shot O'Reilly a look, then accepted the challenge, moving slowly to the desk, leaning over the keyboard.

"You want me to type her name?" Jessup asked.

"I want you to try," Peter said.

"Dina, right?" Jessup said.

"D-I-N-A."

"C'mon, Peter," Rossi said. "Stop this now."

"It's okay," Jessup said calmly. And with the index finger of his right hand, he pressed the letter D.

It popped up on the computer screen, as he knew it would.

Then he hit the I.

Same result.

"No," Peter said.

Next the N.

"Stop!" Peter's chest was suddenly constricting, his breathing heavy and hard. "I've changed my mind."

But Jessup shook his head. "Too late," he said, pressing the letter A.

There on the computer screen, the name Dina, exactly as typed.

"Sorry," Jessup said.

It was as if all life had been drained, and the gun was too heavy to hold. Staring at the name on the monitor in disbelief, Peter dropped his arms to his sides. The Beretta slipped out of his hand, falling to the floor.

O'Reilly moved quickly, slamming him up against the wall, slapping on the cuffs.

Rossi retrieved the weapon. "It's not even loaded," she said, looking into Peter's face for an answer, a reason.

Just confusion.

"You okay?" O'Reilly asked, turning toward his partner.

Jessup answered with an embarrassed nod, the

adrenaline cooling, as Rossi gently led Peter out of the office.

"I don't understand," Peter whispered, tears coming to his eyes now, finally free.

"Everything will be okay," she told him as they stepped through the doorway.

Behind him, he was pretty sure he heard O'Reilly comment to Jessup, "The guy's fucking insane."

It took every ounce of will to keep from smiling, but that was so what Peter wanted to hear.

His only chance at revenge.

The best defense in the world.

About the Author

Jonathan Baine is a pseudonym for an award-winning independent filmmaker who lives in New Haven, Connecticut, with his wife and two dogs. For more information, visit his Web site at www.jonathanbaine.com.

Penguin Group (USA) Inc.
is proud to present
GREAT READS—GUARANTEED

**We are so confident you will love
this book that we are offering a
100% money-back guarantee!**

If you are not 100% satisfied with
this publication, Penguin Group (USA) Inc.
will refund your money!
Simply return the book before
March 2, 2007 for a full refund.

**With a guarantee like this one,
you have nothing to lose!**